A Platonic Love

Paul Alexis

Translated By Richard Robinson

Sunny Lou Publishing Company
Portland, Oregon, USA
http://www.sunnyloupublishing.com

2nd Edition: June 15, 2025
Original Publication Date: May 18, 2021

ISBN: 978-1-955392-77-8

* * *

This translation, from French, is based on the Librairie des
Publications, Paris, 1886, edition of
Un amour platonique.

(This novella was also entitled the *Journal of Mr. Mure*, or
Journal de M. Mure, in the 2nd edition of an earlier
publication of several novellas by Paul Alexis, by the
publisher G. Charpentier, Paris, 1880.)

Contents

Foreword...5

Chapter 1...9

Chapter 2...15

Chapter 3...19

Chapter 4...27

Chapter 5...35

Chapter 6...43

Chapter 7...49

Chapter 8...53

Chapter 9...61

Chapter 10...75

Chapter 11...79

Chapter 12...93

Chapter 13...103

Chapter 14...119

Foreword

Of all the novellas or works of Paul Alexis that I have read or translated, – and I can count them on the fingers of one hand – *A Platonic Love* is my favorite.

Paul Alexis' touch is fine, his style is deft. This book is elegantly written, nostalgic, and masterful. If it weren't for the Naturalist moniker that often gets attached to him – by literary historians – I'd say he was Romantic. The last thing that comes to my mind, when I read him, is Émile Zola, the man he admired, the man he was close friends with, the man whose official biography he wrote, the man who, along with himself sometimes, and perhaps for that very association, was so contemned by Léon Bloy.

Paul Alexis is not very well known at all in the English-speaking world, nor even in the French one. If I had to compare his style to an author who is much better known today, depending on my audience, I'd point to say F. Scott Fitzgerald, and particularly to this latter's *The Great Gatsby*, which is perhaps more complicated than *A Platonic Love*, – but participates in the same rich and deep feeling of longing, unrequited love, and strong sense of nostalgia for things of the past. Another book or novella that comes to mind is *The Sorrows of Young Werther*, by Goethe, because of the rich Romanticism and unrequited love and longing on the part of the protagonist.

A Platonic Love is so beautifully written and so masterfully executed that it only goes to show just how unfair literary popularity can be – for those who do not have it; it also goes to show just how many jewels and gems are there "free for the taking" as it were, for those readers and students of literature willing to get off their duff (or perhaps on their duff) and spend the time and effort needed to hunt them down and to read them. If you, as the reader, enjoy this story, I encourage you to read also Paul Alexis' *The Misfortune of Mr. Fraque* especially; possibly also his *The End of Lucie Pelegrin*, this latter work, not so much for the characters, who are coarser and *feel* less, but for the general feeling of nostalgia for a time gone by, that pervades the novella.

Besides nostalgia, there is also something edgy in *A Platonic Love* that might resonate more with today's readers (for better or for worse), some *little* something that flickers and flashes every now and again and palpitates just beneath the surface of the page, close enough to the surface that a keen reader will detect it in the main character. But it is so ephemeral and fleeting, like an autumn breeze on the cheek or a butterfly with horns on the leaf. Mr. Mure's love for Helen is so enduring and endearing, so constant and so pure, but also so concealed – that if ever there was a story of unrequited, true love – innocent love between two friends who have known each other since at least one of them was a child – this is it. His is a Platonic love that could have been more than that – something more modern – if only the stars had lined up right and remained in their positions for a little while longer, long enough for him to gain his courage perhaps, or summon his demons, and if only Mr. Mure, the good Mr. Mure, the Mr. Mure fifteen years Helen's senior had been a little less mature, a little less honorable, and a little more selfish than he was. If he had acted like most people today act, in other words. One will be hard pressed to find a Mr. Mure in the literature of today, or in real life. Today, among millennials, Generation Xers and Yers, and whatever else we have or call them nowadays, – because everything is so hyper labeled and packaged these days – the modern generations weaned on video games and the Internet, Twitter, transgenderism, and online pornography, whereas the baby boomers before them were weaned on black-and-white television, landlines, Playboy, and cornflakes, – one will be hard pressed to find one person among them who might believe that someone like Mr. Mure ever existed. Such skepticism, such cynicism, such decadence...

Today, his kind are gone, long gone, arch gone, at least in the near term. And the rest of us, like over-ripe fruit, are just rotting on the branches, or wallowing in the wet dirt beneath the tree, eaten or pushed around by the miserable worms and don't realize it, or don't care, or just don't know what to do about it. It's sad, but things have gone so wrong and so bad so fast in the Occident, that it is hard to see our way back; we are like little Alices in Wonderland or Hansels and Gretels on post-postmodern LSD laced with the will to live and the right to scream and kick in silence. It's not pretty, but that's what we have got right now, and it won't get any better before the trip gets much worse – we'll have to make the best of it or self-combust like warm fertilizer. At least we have this story to read and to enjoy in the meantime.

– Richard Robinson, May 17, 2021

Chapter 1

November 20, 1863.

Today! Before midnight, Miss Helen Derval will be Mrs. Moreau for life.

It's five o'clock in the evening. It's dark outside. I rang twice for the lamp, in vain. Nanon, the maid, will have exited by now; I have just lit a candle while waiting. And I must bother myself again to throw several logs onto the fireplace... Brrr! The cold seizes me, in my bachelor's apartment, alone.

Eight thirty.

My dinner, at home, did not last long.

They, on the other hand, are still at the table. Eating dessert perhaps. The cork from each bottle of champagne pops. I see them, all of them! Old Papa Derval, red in the face like his retired army major's medal, has a tear in his eye. Our president of the tribunal rises, inhales a pinch of snuff, and offers a toast. The indispensable life of the party, Mr. de Lancy, makes some jest to amuse the ladies. And she?

She was so small when I went on vacation, hunting at Miramont at my grandmother's place. On Sundays, for mass, the Dervals climbed the steep hill where the village is perched. They stopped by our house. One time, I remember, I had taken her from her wet nurse and held her in my hands. Suddenly, something passed through the diapers and got my fingers wet.

"Oh! that, sir, that's good luck!" the wet nurse told me, taking her back again.

In our garden, around the large buckthorn, she ran, jumping, like a sparrow. And the barrel organ that my grandmother had given to the church as a gift and that the schoolmaster played during mass at eleven o'clock! It had to be placed standing up on the chair right next to the harmonium: she touched it, kicked it with her foot, also wanted to turn the crank. She danced before knowing how to walk. One afternoon when a family of Italians played the harp in front of the house, I still see her: marking time with her foot, jumping, improvising, the adorable steps of a four-year-old dancer who held up her skirts so she wouldn't tread on them. And another day, several years later, her good-natured father, after having threatened to put her in the dark cabinet, for I don't know what foolishness, finished by locking her in a bright cabinet, between two glass doors. She cried at first, then suddenly, with a cry of revolt and triumph that I can still hear:

"Papa, I can see!..."

The truth is that, as a mere child, still in her little dress, she already intimidated me, me, a grown man, a doctor of law, a magistrate, mature and serious for my age. I addressed her formally early on, when I spoke to her, that baby, who played with her dolls at that period, and who, with her fingers sticky with jam, dared to pull on my mutton-chop whiskers.

Nine o'clock

They have left the table by now! Those who were not invited for dinner, arrive. One begins to pile into the salon. The domestics circulate as best they can with their trays. Fortunately, it is no longer customary to dance at wedding parties. Greetings are made, compliments given, people are observed with sidelong glances, while taking punch or sorbets. The men, relegated to the corners, whisper amongst themselves, wipe sweat from their brows; the ladies try to look at themselves in the mirror while passing. The president of the tribunal is on his twenty-fifth pinch of snuff and, in a window embrasure, recites his toast to some newly-arrived guest. Finally the amiable Mr. de Lancy really has to do his utmost to keep people entertained: everyone wishes that it were eleven o'-clock already, the moment of departure for city hall.

One person's name that must often be pronounced, it's mine. I can almost hear them! With each new arrival: "And Mr. Mure?" "How is it I cannot find Mr. Mure?" "Is it possible something has happened to the dear Mr. Mure?" Everyone knows that it is I who brought this marriage together. Then, Moreau, in that dry tone of voice of his, with his ceremonious attitude of a starchy magistrate, informs them that a fit of gout keeps me at home in my room. And there are sympathetic exclamations: "How's that! the gout at his age!" "But Mr. Mure is not old!" "Forty years old... at most!" "Hopefully he hasn't got something serious!" while her father, Derval, with moist eyes, sighs and makes gestures with his arms towards heaven to indicate that my absence is a setback to his perfect happiness. But Moreau informs them that I have been afflicted with gout for some time now; and, in the same tone that he spoke, when presiding over the last assizes, – "Accused: you have three days to submit an appeal," – he reveals to them that I had just spent some time at Vichy. – "But there's better than Vichy for that affliction," shouted someone immediately with a knowing air: "There's Contrexeville!" – "Ah! yes, Contrexeville! in my case, however..." And there they go talking about spas, alkaline baths and sulfurous baths, dips in the sea, casinos, toilettes, roulette, concerts, actresses, bankers, the stock market, politics, etc. I'm completely forgotten, until the arrival of some latecomer.

Ten o'clock.

Everyone has arrived now.

Ah well, if I showed up?... My tails! my varnished boots! my combed beard!... At the moment when they aren't expecting anyone, I would stupefy them by demonstrating that I no more suffer from the gout than Moreau does. Anyone else might have neglected the jabot lace on the shirt by now. But, I am Mr. Mure...

Eleven o'clock.

Too late!

I have just heard the sound of many carriages rolling by, at the end of the Avenue. The wedding party arrives at the city hall. Me, I'm suffering. I have something that feels like a lead bullet there, somewhere, in my chest. They've taken their wedding vows.

Chapter 2

The following day, November 15.

Bad night. A sleep interrupted by idiotic dreams.

I was alone with her, me, in a passenger car carrying us to Italy. She, still a child, mischievous, playful, leaned imprudently out the door. I wanted to hold her back: she pinched me and pulled on my beard... – then she began to turn the handle of a shiny harmonium sitting next to her on the bench. Suddenly, no more harmonium; and, what did I see shining there in its place, but Moreau's pince-nez. Then... I don't know anymore. A nightmare. A tiresome cloud made of the smoke of baroque imaginings. I'm still affected by it. Also, given that they should be in Nice, or Menton, or Genoa by now, I walk outside to get a bit of fresh air on the Avenue. Then I will go and read my evening journals at the reading room.

Same day.

No news about Mexico. – Annuity rates, low. – Flipped through an interesting variety of *Debates* on the museums of Florence and Venice. Why did this untoward father Derval shove a dispatch from his daughter under my nose?

Cannes, 3:47. All goes well. Will write tomorrow... Helen.

Ah, yes, excellent man, I found a husband for your daughter, and you are grateful: but leave me alone!

I will never step into the reading room again.

If he gets it into this head, in the coming days, to come and show me the fine scribblings of Mrs. Moreau, my door will be shut to him.

December 15.

For three weeks now, father Derval hasn't left my side as it were. She has sent him five other dispatches, from Rome, from Naples, from Milan. Finally, just yesterday, a two-page letter with a *post-scriptum* by her husband. I know it by heart.

This evening, she returns by the last train.

Same day.

There was a delay. In the deserted waiting room, her father and I, we paced up and down for a long time without saying anything. Then the good man wanted to sit, and he fell asleep at my side. Me, I mechanically looked at an immense geographical map on the wall in front of me, taking great interest, without knowing why, in the large boot of Italy, plunged in the pale azure of the Mediterranean. Suddenly a telegraph bell rang, signaling the train's approach. Her father got up and rubbed his eyes. And me, however, who had not fallen asleep, it felt like I had just woken up as well.

It was as if I was more alive. We were permitted to cross over the tracks. The train entered heavily into the station, making the turntables vibrate. Already the employees, lantern in hand, cried out in a sluggish manner the name of the station. The car doors, here and there, opened. All of a sudden, at the last revolution of the train wheel, I saw her, her first, already standing on the walkway, impatient.

"Papa!..."

And before Mr. Derval had finished embracing her:

"There you are! Good evening Mr. Mure!..."

The rapid feeling of the tip of her gloved hand in mine. Her large, velvety, and expressive eyes, in the shadows. A smile. Two or three small slaps on her traveling outfit. Around her, in the night, something mysterious, attractive and subtle, emanated from her person. And then nothing! She felt so tired that she had already departed in a carriage with her father.

Then there was Moreau, with luggage tickets in hand:

"You, you will wait to help me unload the trunks, yes?... It shouldn't take long; but here, hold my cane, my umbrella... There you go! oh, and this bag as well."

Chapter 3

April 1865.

One thing surprises me and saddens me. In less than eighteen months, Helen has turned her back on the society of X***. One by one, the women, without apparent motive, have distanced themselves from her, left her in a void.

Today, she is no longer in contact with some of the wives of counsellors, colleagues of mine and Moreau's. And what contact! Visits, two or three times a year, of great ceremony when Court resumes, for example. Most often, a simple exchange of cards.

It's my fault. I should never have left it in the hands of her husband or father, when she debuted last winter in society. The "society" of X! What a joke!...

It would have required changing my behavior, my entire manner of being.

Firstly, to order my dress shirts from Paris, a suit from a good tailer, etc..

Secondly, to have myself invited to Mrs. de Lancy's, who pretends to galvanize the local aristocracy by giving dances every two weeks.

With more hair, real or fake, several years younger, the desire to go and spend time chatting about a thousand pleasant trivialities with the ladies, with a solid waltzer's ham, I could have helped Helen avoid much of the frivolity. But, if I had possessed those qualities, wouldn't Mrs. Moreau today have called herself Mrs. Mure?

Eight days later.

Old Colonel Blimp of a father Derval, leave me be!

The other morning, at the end of the Avenue, all of a sudden I had both my arms held back from behind.

"Prisoner! I won't let you go!... Let's go walk around town together."

And, seeing that that didn't please me all too much, he said:

"Let's go get an absinthe, Goodness gracious!... You can't refuse me that, young man..."

He was brisk and bright like the morning air. While leaving the Avenue, he asked the guard on duty, an old soldier, about the gun he was holding and began speaking about Africa: "When I was on the battlefield of Médéa..." From the end of his cane, he applied, in passing, a small tap on the behind of a young maid who, carrying a basket, was making her way towards the station. In the suburb, in front of an old theatre bill, it was an uninterrupted firing of puns. Then, impatient at the end of all this, not having fallen asleep until three o'clock in the morning the night before, because I was thinking about his daughter! I let it all out. But, – since I knew him well – with circumspection, little by little, juxtaposing the facts.

In the beginning there was only stupefaction and incredulity on his part. Ah! yes, well... What did I just say? His daughter! To begin with, was she not the only progeny of his, him, Théodore Derval, superior officer of the African Army, Changarnier's ex-aide-de-camp, thirty-seven years of service, nineteen campaigns, eleven wounds!

And then, wasn't she educated at Saint-Denis, his daughter. Among the daughters of majors, colonels, generals as well as simple legionnaires, a perfect education! at once egalitarian and hierarchical!... And, I knew her well myself! From nine years old, when she had lost her mother, to nineteen years of age, hadn't Helen profited, up there in Paris, from the lessons of top-rate teachers in the capital!... Leaving the suburb, her father and I found ourselves now under the hundred-year-old elms of the boulevard Saint-Louis.

Fortunately, nobody was walking there. He, with the blood already gone to his head, raised his voice louder and louder, not letting me get a word in edgewise. – History! geography! drawing! religion! music! embroidery! dance! literature! nothing had been neglected: his daughter was perfect! The daughter of a marshal of France was not raised better than his daughter! X*** (and he struck the stones of the city rampart with his cane), X*** was not worthy of this pearl, which would have shined with all its brilliance in the faubourg Saint-Germain, any more than this civvy of a Moreau was worthy of her for a wife... But, great balls of fire! those men of the court, "all pen pushers!" had chicken blood in their veins... It was me who pushed for this marriage!... Was I telling him everything, at least? What's more, no matter what happened, his daughter could not have committed the least shadow of a wrong. He could still see her, last winter, entering for the first time, dressed up for the ball at the de Lancy's house: a beauty! a queen, my god! Her shoulders made him forget that he was her old man! What palpitations he felt under his evening jacket hearing the men and women murmuring: "the beautiful Mrs. Moreau!" – Here, I thought he was going to cry. But we had arrived at the gate of the Platform. A little out of breath, he stopped walking, his hand holding onto the railing that encircled the decorative fountain – a jet of water coming out of an iron basket. Through the mist of the water, between the trunks of young sycamore trees, the view of the town – which, through the gap in the rue de la Comédie, appeared stacked up and asleep at our feet, under an ardent sun already high in the sky – brought him suddenly to the height of exasperation. And, menacing the town with his fist, as if X*** in its entirety was his daughter's enemy, he spoke.

"That's where they are," he exclaimed, "those women!... At this moment, they've hardly opened their eyes and stretched in their beds... the bunch of bitches!..."

And, all the while as we walked along the boulevard Saint-Jean, I had to listen to the scandalous chronicles of X***. A bunch of stories, well known, whether true or false, in circulation about this woman or that woman. Didn't Mrs. "so and so" make her husband the laughing stock of town? And Mrs. B., the wife of a judge of the court, hadn't we heard enough gossip about her, under the sub-prefect before last. Mrs. V., the wife of a rich banker, openly and publicly a crazy bitch in heat! And Mrs. N. N. – a marquise that one, an authentic marquise, didn't she keep in her house, for five years, under the same roof as her very husband, a poor Corsican student! And the wife of K., who was seen everywhere with officers of various rank! Mrs. C., surprised one morning with a priest! And Mrs. D.! and Mrs. E.! and F.! etc., etc... He wouldn't stop. Nobility, magistrature, the bar, civil service, commerce, women of all levels of society, paraded before us: the entire enumeration of X***. Sometimes, on the mention of a name, his hand pointed out, above the ivy-covered ramparts, the chestnut trees of some antique house. All accepted, however, received everywhere, welcomed with open arms; protected, this one here by her name, that one there by her fortune, and that other one by the force of habit, by indifference, by the *esprit de corps* of a rather skeptical society fundamentally, which is only straight-laced at the surface.

"Well, and my daughter!... what is it to me, me, if she no longer frequents all those...?"

Our walk around the town came full circle. We found ourselves again at beginning of the Avenue. He was still red in the face, exuding large beads of sweat, breathing like a bull, walking for a long time without saying a word. Then suddenly he stopped to wipe his brow. Then, turning towards me, and with a tone of reproach, he spoke.

"I'm obliged to take a foot bath when I get

home... All that was quite useless."

And pointing out to me with his hand the balcony of the de Lancy's house:

"There is the proof that you exaggerate: Mrs. de Lancy is always there for her..."

Same year.

Moreau himself is nothing but an indifferent person.

She has nobody but me. To be useful to her without her knowing about it, to stop at nothing. To act like a secret policeman, if necessary, and to proceed methodically.

Firstly, life in the small town is transparent as glass. In X*** there are no secrets.

Everything happens on the Avenue: the *Nobles'* circle, the *Lawyers'* circle, the *Business* circle, the *Gascony* circle, the *Education* circle, and that of the *Public Order*, and the *Republican*, and the *Musical*, and the *Catholic*, and that of the *Carafe* (whose members only drink water!) and the *Babies-Club*, – plus a reading room, – plus fifteen cafés, – plus five tobacco shops, hairdressers, etc., etc... Ah yes, before the door of all these public establishments, from morning to evening, the lazybones, sitting outside on chairs, smoking, yawning, stretching their arms, not knowing how to kill the time, but looking, observing, communicating what they had observed, then commenting, criticizing, conjecturing... Their natural malignity makes them malign sometimes, and at other times, divine... So, I must always have my ears cocked and take advantage of this entirely organized system of espionage.

Secondly, I'm familiar enough with everyone to be able to visit them at all hours of the day. My capacity as an old bachelor authorizes me to sit down frequently at their table.

Same year.

Mrs. de Lancy, Helen's last friend.

I run into her, at every instant, in the street or on the promenades, on the arms of her husband, both of them walking very fast, with large strides, – like completely young people in a hurry: him, his nose in the air, completely lacking in manners, – her, tall, slender, extraordinarily thin, pale, with drawn features, her mouth imperceptibly askew; in sum, a strange woman, but distinguished, in her gothic style of dress that, exaggerating her thinness, makes her look vaguely like some medieval chatelaine. She doesn't look a day over twenty. But Henry, her oldest scatterbrained son, has already been denied his high--school diploma five times.

Parisian, last descendent of an old family that shined at the time of the Crusades, raised in the faubourg Saint-Germain, at a distant relative's, a canoness.

Married, without a dowry, by Mr. de Lancy, thus without fortune: a marriage of love! – For several years subsisting on love and water at room temperature, in Paris, while Mr. de Lancy solicited in vain an appointment as consul. – Then, one fine day, the death of a filthy rich uncle, in X***. Three million francs! – So to hell with the consulship! – And they arrived one fine morning in X*** in full mourning, and impatient to enjoy their inheritance.

The mourning did not last long. The inheritance continues still.

Chapter 4

April, 1866.

This afternoon, towards four o'clock, after Helen had closed the metal gate of their house behind her, and when she had gone outside dressed in her spring dress, I saw her. Without her suspecting it, me, from the skylight of a room on the fourth floor, where my old books and a pile of wretched papers slumber, I can see beyond the limits of town, above the Rotunda and large fountain, as far as the new houses in the neighborhood of the train station.

She walked briskly at first; but, upon reaching the Rotunda, having walked up onto the circular sidewalk of the monumental fountain, a slowing of pace; then a short stop, to re-button up her glove. A rider was approaching at that moment at a short trot. Her tilted head did not budge, any more than her pretty pearl-grey umbrella. Then, the rider having passed, she descended the sidewalk and entered town. But the rider, having turned round in his saddle and then also his horse, watched her. I recognized the young Count de Vandeuilles.

Along the Avenue, she went slowly. When she passed in front of me, skirting the house, from my mansard window I could no longer see her. The time seemed long to me.

What if she was coming up!

But I knew that she never came up to my

place. Then, from my window, I picked up on her again on the promenade, appearing and disappearing among the green tufts of young plane trees, moving farther away with a supple, rhythmic pace, as revealed by the small, graceful back-and-forth movement of her umbrella. Then, she was no longer between the two green, close rows of plane trees, but instead a small, pearl-grey mark, ever gay to behold, imperceptible in the end, but visible. And when, after having finally lost sight of her, I came back from the window with a terrible case of torticollis, my thoughts continued to follow her.

She goes out like this everyday, at the same hour, from Moreau's Swiss chalet, which from here looks like a child's plaything, with its high, ridiculous roof coming down low and its red paint job, heavy-handed in all and coarsely made. Irreproachable in bearing, noble and charming, better positioned than others and with a Parisian cachet that nobody forgives her for, she enters the town.

In town, she knows exactly where she is: X***, every single resident, knows her now and does not like her. Here come the women, right in front of her, who no longer accept her visits. They stare at her, they search her face, they undress her with their eyes; then, when she has passed, the same women turn around, not having gotten enough of her, as if they were looking at some curious animal... Here's the wife of the public prosecutor now, arriving from afar, with the marquise N. N. Those two, at least, greet her: she still exchanges cards with one of them! the other, the marquise, proposed to her, four days ago, to accompany her on a trip to the baths at Uriage! Ah well, no! both of them turn their heads away, taking the other path of the promenade... And now it's necessary that she step aside to let the young Mrs. Jauffret pass. Having left her village to marry a young poseur who comes up only to her shoulders, this tall asparagus shoot does not fill out her dresses even, but would like to take up all the public walkway... And that's just the women! With her passage, there's some agitation in front of the cafés and circles: those who hang about outside alert those who are within; the readings of journals are interrupted; clusters of hatless heads appear, together with hands that hold a billiard stick or cards spread out like a fan... When they see her come, the officers of number 217 throw back their shoulders, stroke their mustaches, risk a wink. More insolent still, our pretentious toffs and little noblemen fix their eyes on her, looking down their noses at her. And it is not rare for bands of eight or ten students, dropouts, good for nothings who cut school, to walk obstinately beside her, while holding obscene conversations out loud. Finally, when nobody is in vicinity, when the public path is free of people, at the very end of those roads where the grass grows tall and where the houses, with their doors and windows closed, seem asleep, she still feels that she's in a hostile atmosphere: watched by eyes that see through walls, pointed at with fingers, but not invisible fingers, put off balance even by the cobblestones, which are bumpier for her delicate foot, desirous of seeing her stumble, as all the city is.

So what does she come to town for? Every afternoon, around four o'clock, what necessity is there for her to expose herself like this, defenselessly, to the animosity of X***! Doubtless, if I dared to interrogate her, she would not tell me the real reason: maybe she would not admit it to herself even! But I know her well, me; moreover, I know now the itinerary that she follows each day, the streets she passes through, the stretches of sidewalk she selects, the purveyors of goods she stops at and buys from, including the confectioner where sometimes she eats a *gateau*, when her promenade has no other pretext; and I understand her! At twenty years old, a grown woman, she's still the little girl who "wanted" so imperiously to be allowed to turn the barrel organ at church, and who, when her father closed her in between the two glass doors of the cabinet, in tears, she suddenly let out a cry of defiance: "Papa, I can see!" This willful character, ever ready to revolt, which the education of Saint-Denis left in tact and which for all the hatred that the town shows her, holds her up at least, allows her to get by. That's why, each day, the hour arrives when Helen feels the need to penetrate X*** not out of idleness nor out of any need to go shopping, not to eat a *gateau*; – but because her presence must cry out to X***: "Here I am! and what have you got to say for yourself? You continue to detest me! Ah, well, as you can see, my hair is no more poorly done than yours! My complexion has not yellowed! What do you think of my new dress? Take good note that my happiness is complete!"

There I was, deep in reflection, resting on my elbows, in front of my mansard window, with those wretched papers of mine. All of a sudden, on the other path of the Avenue, I saw Helen again, walking at a slow pace. She was going back home for dinner. A little behind her, Mr. de Vandeuilles, who had dismounted his horse, walking along with the de Lancy boy. Monocled, the two young noblemen held her in their sights. The de Lancy boy, bursting out in laughter, a bit drunk, pointed at her at each instant with his stick.

At least, Mr. de Vandeuilles held back the lout's arm.

* * *

Rediscovered after digging through my old papers, I had written the following, a long time a go, to a Parisian, a good, adventurous, but intelligent fellow, who, feeling cramped in Europe, went to New York to die of yellow fever:

> *... Take a foreshortening of your faubourg Saint-Germain, a miniature of your Chausée-d'Antin, add a smidgen of Marais, add a bit of the tail end of Belleville; don't mix them up, – on the contrary, separate them into four distinct parts, as diminutive as diverse worlds, all behind the times by one century, rubbing shoulders without blending, viewing each other with hostility, frittering away the time by spying on one another, envying and being envied, gossiping; add many churches, parishes, chapels; an archbishop; canons, parish priests, vicars, monks, nuns*

*with all types of headdress, Capuchin nuns and monks, Jesuit monks and nuns; brotherhoods of white, black, blue, grey penitents, etc., etc.; now, if all that can be contained in a fold of earth in the middle of a hilly, but rough, country, made dreary everywhere by small dusty olive trees, calcined in the summer by the sun, frozen in the winter by the mistral; and if the grass pushes up between the pavement as in the cemetery; if the fountains are without water; if the spirit does not roam through the streets; if the ideas are antediluvian; if... I could multiply the 'ifs' indefinitely... well, my dear friend, that's X***!*

Hold on now! Thursday, eight o'clock in the evening, an admirable end to a summer day. Arranged in a circle in the middle of the Avenue, up where the officer's café is, the regiment band plays the White Lady. *From the balcony of the house where I was born, my friend, we watch. At our feet, the two paths of the promenade, lined with chairs occupied by ladies all dressed up, children, gentlemen. Other families, also dressed up, are seated on the ground in between. But, after studying closely all those chairs, we will discover distinct categories, brusk and profound differences; we will arrive at tracing a map, yes, a real and curious map of social geography, with lines of certain demarcation. For example, that doorman's wife who is so lanky, so bony, so poorly dressed, with the prominent and mountainous nose, has no doubt in her mind that we will mistake her for a natural frontier... And a little farther down, – yes, there, precisely! – that clan of young women and young girls, some of them hideous, others charming, but all seeming to belong to one family, they are the Israelites: neither the nobility nor the magistrature greets them, and they call them "the Jews"! Apart from the large balls held in the sub-prefecture, – a neutral and banal terrain like the middle causeway, – they only go to the intimate parties thrown by the wife an oil merchant.*

This scrap of yellow paper brings me back in time by many years. I had just left school, then. My feelings had an exalted verdure that surprises me now. It's true that at that time I was not without some literary desires, I read Balzac and Stendhal, I knew Musset by heart. In my letters to friends, as with my first pleadings at the assizes, I strove to show some style. As also, in the evening, in bed, before falling asleep, erecting great houses of cards: Paris! Successes as a publicist and as an orator! Loves in the manner of Rastignac, in the manner of Julien Sorel![1] money! sensual pleasure! glory! power! Today, having become pragmatic, calm, sensical, I could not write those lines again.

Or, at a minimum, I would no longer amuse myself with the futility of drawing a small sketch of the regiment band on Thursdays. I would no longer spend my time enumerating the town clerics. Now also, I have stopped getting upset at the mistral; I have come to terms with the "small dusty olive trees"; and the grass in the streets, the impracticable pavement, the fountains without water, the inhabitants' common vulgar spirit, and I have grown accustomed to it. Apart from these nuances in detail or form, the result of a difference in years, the basis of my observations at that time were correct.

Me, in and of myself, I have changed: but X*** is still X***!

---

[1] Julien Sorrel: the protagonist of Stendhal's *Le Rouge et le Noir.*

Chapter 5

One Sunday.

Mrs. de Lancy attended Helen's wedding, without having known her as a young girl. But father Derval and Mr. de Lancy were from the same circle. A certain intimacy existed all the same between them. Moreover, this Mr. de Lancy was so affable, so superficial, so stupid, and so fine a fellow all at the same time. Despite everything, a nice fellow! Nobility subsists in him: he is full of himself and his superiority, the superiority of those of his caste looking down on those who are ignoble. But for all his nobility, he cannot resist a glass of absinthe, the excitement of a night of gambling, the power and impetus of a party, even the simple irresistibility of a joke to play, the eccentricity of a commercial traveler or the folly of schoolboy on a day off. Didn't I see him just the other day, at the barbershop, speaking informally with the boy who was cutting his hair, daubing soap on the snout of the shop's cat, and with his open hand giving the owner large pats on the back! He may be growing gray, be fifty years old, have crow's feet about the eyes, with rheumatisms: but he's every bit like his scatterbrained son. What's more they are both on familiar terms, have the same tailor, lead the same life, frequent the same circle nowadays, play with the same cards, bet on each other and act as each other's bank[2]; at the ballroom, they dance with the same fervor and, during the hour of cotillon, bump into each

---

[2]act as each other's bank: from French *se font des banquo*.

other sometimes, father and son, at the knees of the same woman. With that, Mr. de Lancy passes for an excellent husband; the father, the son, and the mother accompany each other to noon mass.

Mrs. de Lancy, herself, has one passion: to receive visitors! In the winter, at her mansion; in the summer, at the tumbledown cottage next to the farm and flanked by a dovecote that is decorated with the name Chateau de Lancy, – she must throw parties. It is in this particular way that the thirst for pleasure, that is characteristic of her family, manifests itself in her. Her husband, a sanguine *bon vivant*, would satisfy more cheaply this need for activity and agitation which remained as imperious in him as in his son. But she, who was somewhat flat chested, slender and pale, nervous, of noble stock, having set foot in childhood on the sill of veritable Parisian society, – was it any surprise that, from the moment she felt herself immersed in the golden bath of fortune, she should want to enjoy the refinements of her nature? She had to remain what she was: religiously elevated, honest by circumstance and by temperament, married to the man she merited, everything leads me to believe she is still one of the most honest women of X***. On the other hand, honesty, religion, love of a husband, often, in life, are exhausted in the long run! Her crazy love of society preserved Mrs. de Lancy, just as others are kept in tact by their aptitude to make jams.

June 2, 1866.

For an entire winter, I listened to Helen who

never stopped talking about Mrs. de Lancy. Even, at one period, it was by her first name: Blanche here! Blanche there!... But after a while no more talk of "Blanche"... After several days, I noticed that each time I mentioned the name of Mrs. de Lancy, Helen's face darkened. Then, yesterday evening, at the chalet, I wanted to get to the bottom of it.

We were quite hot, the three of us, while dining. With her rosy skin, a little moist, lowered eyes, silent and not listening to us, Moreau and me, she peeled her strawberries slowly. All of a sudden, she looked at us:

"What do you say we all go outside to have our coffee?"

"Outside or inside," said Moreau with an indifferent gesture.

We went outside onto the terrace, then, to sit around the stone table. The coffee was steaming in our three glasses. Moreau, already sitting back in his rustic armchair, was lighting a cigar. The day was dying, and there was a great calm in the air.

"Not a leaf on the trees is moving!" I exclaimed. There we were, completely enjoying the beautiful weather...

Then, after an instant, I said:

"We spent some fine evenings here, last summer!... Mrs. de Lancy visited sometimes, often..."

At that moment, Helen passed the sugar bowl to me with a certain violence.

"Here! have some sugar... Have some sugar!"

Her voice vibrated, imperative and indignant, brutal. Saddened to have touched a sore spot, and feeling troubled myself, I continued to search about in the sugar bowl, with the silver tongs, for a long second, for a very small morsel of sugar. Then I stole a glance at her. She had already regained her composure. She emptied her glass of coffee in a single draught, held it in the air for just a moment, put it down with an assured gesture. Under the transparency of her white corsage, her bosom respired, broadly and unrestricted. Once again, she had forgotten us, Moreau and me. What was she thinking about? She seemed to be listening. From time to time, the sound of a locomotive's whistle reached us from the station.

And Moreau, who had brought his journals outside with him, skimmed through them. At each instant, there was a small rustle of paper as it unfolded. As well, that evening, expansive in his manner, he included us in his reading, dropping clipped phrases: "Price increase, 30 centimes... Excellent attitude on the part of Austria... Jules Favre comes here to plead before the Court... Remedy for phylloxera... Well what do you know, our old public prosecutor is nominated in Rennes." In a neighboring garden, a nightingale let out two or three velvety notes, at times.

Finally, it was night already. But the atmosphere was so pure, the moon beneath the trees of the garden was rising so round and bright that Moreau could have continued his reading. The journal that he was holding slipped through his fingers onto the ground, without his budging to pick it up again. He had fallen asleep.

Helen looked at him. Her face, impenetrable and hard at this moment, must have contained a thought she did not communicate to me.

"Look at that! He's snoring," was all she said. And she looked at me.

"Why don't you and I walk around for a bit," she added. "Come on..."

I followed her. The gravel on the paths made a crackling sound under our feet. We turned our backs on the chalet, embedded deeper and deeper in the copse that extends from the terrace to the tall fence bordering the route. Subdued by the low branches, the moon produced scattered drops of yellow light that was filtered here and there through the leaves. And I found myself in one of those moments in life when one sees oneself clearly. My heart was heavy. Temptations took hold of me: there, in the shadows, to prostrate myself at her feet, to kiss the edge of her dress, to ask her pardon! Pardon to have loved her and to have been mistaken, to have been the cause of her unhappiness in life, for having played a part in her marriage to the man who was not suitable for her, the man who was good only for stoking my unconscious jealousy, and my egoism.

Already my lips parted:

"Helen!... Helen!"

But she let out a small cry:

"Ah!"

And she added gaily:

"Don't you see? … But untangle me..."

A hazel tree branch was stuck in her hair. Then she spoke again. They really needed to cut back these hazel trees; all that was poorly maintained; she would consider making the pruner come out here. She didn't like the thin spider webs that one felt on one's face suddenly either, when walking through the paths where nobody had passed all winter. She even thought about some embellishments. Here, a greenhouse would be good; they absolutely had to enlarge the little body of water, change the loose stones. And each one of these phrases acted as a calmative and a balm to me. I felt my heart grow lighter. She was growing accustomed then to her situation! No more extreme resolutions to fear on her part. My God! One grows accustomed to everything here. Mrs. de Lancy, like the others, turned her back on her: never mind! Helen would resign herself to isolation. Too proud not to rise to the occasion, she would arrive little by little at relying on herself. And I saw myself already passing an infinity of other evenings with her: during the winter, in the chalet's salon, in a corner by the fire; during the summer, in the embellished garden; – Moreau out of the way, forgotten, indifferent, fallen asleep; – and she, resigned as now, sweet and touching, a little sad.

"The sweet smell of the seringa!" she exclaimed.

We were at the edge of the garden, before the tall railings, covered by a curtain of verdure. And she took the trouble to cut off a long branch of seringa in full flower.

"Help me..."

She picked jasmine too. Then, casting aside the foliage, holding onto the thick iron bars with both hands, she looked out onto the road.

The road, in the moonlight, was very white. Here and there, on the edges, small piles of stones, symmetrical; and, at intervals, the long telegraph poles lined up neatly. Nobody passed. But as the night was very calm, the murmur of little bells, perpetually stirred, arrived from some distant carriage. In the past, before the invention of the railroad, it was by this road that one traveled to Paris. Paris was then somewhere, over there, beyond the horizon, very faraway. Paris! The magic city, as attractive for the unhappily married woman as for the schoolboy hiding Balzac inside his desk and dreaming of a literary career! Paris! Still clinging to the railings like bars on a prison window, Helen sought I do not know what, with fixed gaze:

"Are you coming?" I implored timidly.

"No! leave me... I'm looking at something."

No matter how wide I opened my eyes, I could not see anything at first. Then, however, on the road, an imperceptible cloud of dust. The cloud grew larger and got closer, very fast, with the sound of horses galloping. In no time at all, the rider was before us. I recognized Mr. de Vaudeuilles.

At ten paces from us, the young count had stopped his horse. He slowly rolled a cigarette, appearing to concentrate all his attention on doing it well, and not noticing us. Then, Helen turned away from the railings precipitously.

"Come on... Let's go back."

And when we passed over the terrace, where Moreau, in his armchair, the journal at his feet, snored now like an organ pipe, she touched me nervously on the shoulder:

"Shh! don't wake him."

Chapter 6

Several days later.

What a blow!... Helen is the talk of the town.

The young count de Vaudeuilles had "abducted" her. She had been his mistress for some time, according to what was said. Yesterday evening, they took the express train for Paris.

Two days later.

She wrote to me.

A simple letter. Several lines scribbled in pencil, from the train.

She does not even mention the name of her husband. A word of disdain and contempt for the city. Then, she speaks to me about her father to whom she will write a letter later. She charges me with being the first person to announce the thing to her father "adroitly." She ends with this ironic phrase: "It's a painful task, which will perhaps be more painful for you than for any other person, but I cannot ask anyone else but you."

And she signs her name.

There's a post scriptum:

"P.S. – If my words are a little *tremulous*, that is only because of the jolts of the express train that carries me. But my heart, itself, does not tremble. –

I'm in love for the first time in my life."

The whole thing, dropped into the mailbox at Dijon.

"Dijon!... Ten-minute stop! Buffet!..."

A night of insomnia, that same summer.

I was suffocating in my bed, unable to read, unable to fall asleep. There I am at my desk, half naked, in shirt sleeves. The window is open. In the blued window pane of the library, I apperceived a thin crescent moon. I am still suffocating.

Helen is in the arms of another man...

* * *

A long time before that. My grandmother's carriage had come to wait for me at the train station. From the running board of the old jalopy, it was a single jump into the car. Tom, the imposing guard dog, as tall as a small donkey, wags his tail silently, deigns to move, and greets me. On a coat peg, while passing, I hang my top hat, the top hat of a young deputy public prosecutor who obtained eight days of furlough from his prosecutor, and I don an old straw hat of mine, a little worn out but very suitable for running through the fields in Miramont. And, a little later, there I am in the vast eating hall on the ground floor of my grandparent's house, where I find all my friends and companions waiting for me to sit down at the table. After handshakes, hugs, in the middle of compliments and felicitations, I address myself to

Major Derval: "And my little friend?... where has she gotten off to my little friend?" – "Where in God's name, that little girl!... she will have escaped... she's still on the threshing floor doing somersaults..." And opening the door, the old man was about to go out running without his hat on, very red in the face and shouting: "Helen!... I really need to talk to her boarding school... Helen! Helen!" I restrain him by the arm. "Don't scold her... let me have the pleasure of calling her myself." And I was off, straight for the threshing floor.

The threshing floor seems deserted to me at first. From afar, nothing but the thick strewings of sheaves treaded on all day long by the peasant's two mules. And what remained intact from the top of the pile that pointed at the sky, the all-red sky, still on fire by the sun whose disk, reduced to nothing, had just gone down. "Hold on! she must have gone into the shack... I will surprise her." And, having advanced with precaution, I remove the "*frieze*" thrown over three forks, placed one inside the other. Nothing! Helen was not in the shack. My eyes scan the entire threshing floor, following the undulations of straw ground up by the mules' iron shoes. Nothing but long yellow immobile waves, a sort of fleecy sea frozen in the calm of dusk. All of a sudden, over there, at the other end of the threshing floor, my gaze notices an imperceptible movement. I go there, walking knee-deep in the straw. Helen was there, lying on her back, her body and two arms all covered in the straw, a large pile of it. Nothing but her little face and brown hair stuck out. She didn't hear me coming. And she seemed to me very pale, thinner, with circles under her eyes, almost frightening to see. She was sleeping perhaps, but it was a disquieted sleep: eyes wide open, with fixed regard.

"Helen!"

No response.

"My little Helen!"

She didn't move. And I wasn't but two paces away from her now.

"Ah!" she said suddenly. "Ah, it's you!... you, my good friend!..."

A bound! The pile of straw that was piled on top of her comes streaming off on all sides. And she wraps her arms around my neck, grimping up on me with all her strength. She wasn't kissing me: she was hanging from me, having climbed up along my body, and she was embracing me desperately with her legs. Me, I was kissing her as an older brother who loved his little sister. I covered her cheeks, immediately inflamed, with the "caresses of a wet nurse." I kissed her face also, her beautiful brown hair with wisps of straw mixed in it.

"Look at you all tousled up, my dear... You look beautiful! You have grown since I last saw you!... Are you still being good?"

Then, in order to put her down gently on the ground, I bend down, one knee in the straw.

"There! Now you must come have some supper... Your papa will be upset, you are all covered in straw... You look like something the cat dragged in! Wait... With my little tortoiseshell comb..."

My fingers were already searching into my fob. But as I turn around, I slip on the straw, and I fall down. Then, with my face on a level with her lips, Helen seizes me again. And, all red, choked with a passion of feeling, the little girl of eight years old started laughing and covered me with kisses.

* * *

Helen is in the arms of another man!

Chapter 7

Eighteen months later.

An old uncle whom I knew since my childhood had a favorite maxim, embellished with a pun, which he repeated incessantly: "Time is a *big meager...*[3]"

Nothing endures. Everything gets sorted out and levelled out in the end. And no matter how much the shock of passions and catastrophes can damage, rend, and crack a life, little by little, a fine, impalpable powder falls on things, dulls the edges, mellows new situations, spreads out everywhere with the uniformity of a salutary patina.

Helen, here, begins to be forgotten.

To begin with, Moreau, since his "misfortune," is recommended for a position in Algiers. His professional instinct straightway advised him that he should change jurisdiction. The magistrature must be taken into consideration! Some highly-positioned relationships that I maintain in the ministry facilitated his relocation to Algeria, where he received more considerable emoluments.

Major Derval himself stupefies me. What a change in that man since the fatal evening when, obeying Helen, I went to apprise him of his daughter's running off! – "Abducted!... Adultery!... In the

---

[3]Time is a big meager: instead of "Time is a great master." In French, *maigre* (meager) half-rhymes with *maîstre* (master).

name of God! my daughter!" – I can still hear his raucous cries. I still see his congested face, the veins in his swollen neck. He tears off his red ribbon in despair. He menaces me with his cane, me, for their marriage! And he wanted to run, in the middle of the night, to Moreau's place "to drag him by the feet somewhere," then to board the train for Paris and surprise the fugitives, blow the brains out of the Count de Vandeuilles... I succeeded in forcefully getting him to bed, where he spent three days between life and death. I didn't leave him, not for a moment. Bleedings, purgatives, emetics, saved him. But he still spent several weeks of dejection and prostration, not daring to go outside, barely responding to me when I came to see him, affecting no longer even to wish to hear the absent person's name pronounced. A short sojourn that I made him take to the countryside produced a happy diversion. Today, the poor man has taken up again one by one his old habits: his circle two times a day, his siesta in the afternoon, his twenty-five-centime *loto* in the evening. He recounts also willingly his memories of Africa: "When I was on the battlefield at Médéa!..."[4] His angry outbursts, always violent and sudden, are subdued and out of earshot. And he takes as many walks along the Avenue as he used to do; with his brisk pace of an old infantryman, touching sometimes the chin of some little housemaid in passing.

Finally, the town. She was much talked about in the first few weeks, the "beautiful Mrs. Moreau," as the topic began to be delved into. She is no longer

---

[4]Médéa: a municipality of Algeria, an important site of battle at the beginning of the French colonization of Algeria in 1830-31.

here! Her grand attitude, her Parisian ease and grace of bearing, her toilette – no longer offended. They know that she will never come back again! Mrs. Jauffret, that long asparagus shoot, is the only one who continues to disparage her. Every now and then, if some *juicy bit* is in the air, it is sure to have come from her. Last winter, wasn't the gossip that the beautiful Mrs. Moreau was at Nice, showing herself off each afternoon on the English Promenade, in the carriage of a Russian prince? The carriage was even hitched up in tandem! Well, as it turns out, little Mr. Jauffret, accompanied by his wife, had lost some several thousand francs in Monaco that he had won here at his circle... This summer, the Jauffrets went to Vichy: on their return wasn't that Mrs. Moreau singing in a provincial troupe, under the name of *"Hellena Dervalli!..."* Now, it's true that the wife of the new curator of waters and forests causes people to talk about her, and that every moment someone is saying: "She will act like Mrs. Moreau one day!" But, at the next scandal, the wife of the curator of waters and forests will be the object of comparison, and it will no longer be a matter of Helen. "Time is a *big meager*."

Consequently, neither the town, nor the husband, nor even the father...

At night.

And what about me?

Chapter 8

Three years later.

I leave the hearing at four o'clock. My doctor recommended exercise to me: I take myself out for a walk.

The day before yesterday, I walked around the town three times, three times, one walk right after the other, like an incarcerated bear walking around in its cage.

Yesterday, I walked for a while on the main road to Paris. It began to rain, and I had to return the way I came. With open umbrella, I stopped for a moment behind the chalet, against the tall railings of the garden, right at the spot where Count de Vandeuilles, on horseback, one certain evening in May, was rolling a cigarette. The chalet belongs today to little Mr. Jauffret, more and more successful at gambling. Drops of rain made a loud monotonous pattering sound on the foliage in the garden. Several yellow leaves were allowed to fall slowly, like golden butterflies, then grew rust-colored here and there on the gravel paths.

Superb weather today. Warm sun. Re-read certain passages from *Madame Bovary* under the centuries-old leafy shade along the Boulevard Saint -Louis. Then, I turned to the left while skirting along in the shadow of a wall. Then, I found myself suddenly before the steep-banked path leading up to the cemetery.

I turned back.

The day after.

I had to go back, to the steep-banked path. How many times already had I not mounted it behind coffins! And one day, me also, I would be carried there, feet forward. Tomorrow perhaps, perhaps in... Let's see! A little calculation! I am forty-five years old: it is certain that I have lived a good deal more than half my life. Well, well! On that day, the same old cypresses will lift their dark green heads above the wall. The crest of the wall will be bristling with the same shards of broken bottle, a petty protection for the majesty of an enclosure for the dead.

Today, alone, escorting no other bier than that which each man bears in himself, and wherein we feel a little bit of ourselves dissolving each day, I walked there. Moreover, to tell the truth, I was less saddened then than at the moment I wrote this phrase. The mugginess that moistened my brow and descended down my spine, was not totally lacking in voluptuousness. My feet were buried in a thick carpet of dust. My eyes blinked in the bright sunlight, and closed. On opening them again, against the tall wall, here and there I saw a leprous moss, burnt and black, a kind of sweat of the dead. But in the fields, a peasant was working the earth while beating his mule: – "Gee up! Lazy bones! Pull hard!" and the babbling of a little bird, which I did nott see, fidgeted in the hedge.

Then, suddenly, through the railings of the gate, the tombs' white stones. After an automatic doff of the hat upon entering, almost immediately, to the right, I was standing before my family's tomb. The name that I bear: "*Mure*," engraved several times in cold stone, preceded by Christian names and followed by two dates: Yes! my father! my mother! With room for me! Bam! suddenly, instead of pitying myself and my family, a distraction: the soil, soaked by the rain, had sunken, and the tombstone leaned to the right! As I was walking away, I was thinking still about the reparation that needed to be done: "I will return with my mason... Provided however that the walls of the vault have not given way like the stone!" Then I found myself in front of the Derval family tomb. And I re-read the inscription that I had written myself: "THÉODORE DERVAL. – *African Army Major, Changarnier's Aide-de-camp, Officer of the Legion of Honor.*"

One year already! He will no longer lose his temper. He will no longer say: "When I was on the battlefield of Médéa!..." For half an hour, after each meal, his complexion, ordinarily red, became scarlet. One evening, after his dinner, instead of going to the circle, he had to take to bed. I was not summoned until the following day. The crisis had passed. – "What a night!" said the maid, shaking her head. They didn't think he was sick. I passed the entire afternoon at his bedside: he wasn't suffering, didn't complain of anything; only, his agitation was extreme. He tossed and turned in bed with each instant, poured his own cold tisane, then talked and talked. He smoked a pipe even. I asked him even if Helen should be alerted. – "Do no such thing! Come on! for a simple indisposition!..." She had just written him the week before, and he read her letter to me. The little girl that she had had with the Count de Vandeuilles was now in her thirteenth month, oh! a magnificent child!... Helen was pregnant again. I' faith, too bad! if it were a boy, Derval would go to Paris to act as godfather to his grandson, and, if need be, he would adopt him one day. Moreover, this Vandeuilles was "an excellent young man" who made his daughter happy. The son-in-law he deserved! And Moreau, "that blasted Moreau," one day or another he'd have to die, dammit!... he, Derval, didn't "give a fig frankly" about public opinion! One of these mornings, he went to "dispose of" his little house, several plots of land that he still owned at Miramont; and, with his four *sous* in hand, he'd thumb his nose at X***, this hole in the ground, this huge bore of a town, this gossip mill. People could say what they wanted, he would go to live in Paris near his daughter, his daughter whom he could not wait to embrace... His daughter! he had forgiven her a long time ago. She had a good reason, after all, not to let herself be annoyed for long by a bunch of hypocrites who had thirty-six lovers for Helen's one... And then, if for nothing else than for his health, Paris, the active life of Paris, was indispensable to him. In X***, he was suffocating! He was not so old, what the devil! he still felt himself to be in good shape. These veterans of the battle of Médéa passed for tough guys! And after having emptied the ashes from his pipe, he got out of bed, put on his slippers and went out on the landing to shout at the maid to make him a cutlet. I left him around evening, very reassured. In the middle of the night, someone came ringing violently at my door: Mr. Derval had passed.

Two days later, the hour of burial having arrived, Helen, in spite of my three dispatches to her, had not responded. On her behalf, I had to send out letters of announcement. I had to lead the mourning with a second cousin of the major, a proprietor of Miramont, come specially for the occasion. A presence from the garrison rendered military honors. A lot of people showed up: members of the circle that Derval belonged to, magistrates, retired officers, the indispensable Mr. de Lancy and his son: all indifferent and curious. I had coached the second cousin in advance; and, when exchanging handshakes, we responded to the silent interrogations that Mrs. Moreau, being very ill, had been unable to come. Their curiosity having been satisfied, the majority of them didn't even attend the church service. At the entrance to the cemetery, the second cousin, having grown very pale, took leave of me brusquely, while thanking me for what I had done for "his relative," me, a simple friend, but he not having set foot in a cemetery for over sixteen years! I would need to excuse him for leaving! the sight of tombs made him feel ill, it was really too much for him! When the soldiers and the priest had distanced themselves as well from the interred, I remained alone. And with each shovelful of dirt by the gravediggers falling dully on top of the casket, I said to myself: "Where is his daughter!... Why didn't she come?... What is she doing at this very moment?"

The following evening, in the reading room, with a copy of the *Official* in hand, instead of reading about the stormy session in the National Assembly, I let myself get carried away with bizarre suppositions. "Is Mr. de Vandeuilles the kind of man to have suppressed my dispatches?" Suddenly, a glimmer of light: "Last year, at this same time, didn't the major speak with me about Tréport, where Helen went with her daughter to bathe in the sea?" Yes, she must have been tranquilly at *Hotel de la Plage* with Mr. de Vandeuilles, thinking that her father was very much alive and kicking! I knew she was the kind of woman not to shed a tear, not to say a word, to jump on the first train that came along, and, after a grueling trip of nineteen hours, to show up with dry eyes, although they were surrounded by a frightening blue circle, and to say "Here I am!" – "But now, it's too late." "I know, but I wanted to come all the same!" – Also, divining the truth, and wanting to avert her, I had telegraphed to Mr. de Vandeuilles, – whom I didn't know at all – to suppress my first dispatches to Helen, to use caution before letting her know the fatal news, finally not to hand over to her, until having sufficiently prepared her for it, an interminably long letter from me, wherein I recounted to Helen everything in great detail; where I filled her in on the last months of her father's existence, his illness, his burial; where I supplicated her, finally, not to return, now that everything had been taken care of, because everyone believed her to be dangerously ill, and that I was there, me, to stand in for her, to execute her intentions, to handle her affairs and to look over her interests of every sort. Two days later, Mr. de Vandeuilles lifted a great weight from me, by letting me know he had received my dispatch and my letter, the both of which had arrived in time.

Finally, this note from her, one week later:

"Thank you for all you have done... You are a true friend. If you take a trip to Paris, come see me. – Helen."

Same year, on vacation.

Last year, around the same time period, I visited Switzerland. This year, I'm not budging from here: I'm a member of the local tourist bureau. Moreover, if I did decide to go anywhere, it would never be to Paris.

"Come see me." To what end? I have nothing to say to her, no more service to render her. Because of the power of attorney she empowered me with, I was able to realize her father's fortune for her. According to her wishes, everything was sold, the farms at Miramont, the house, even the furniture, – all but some souvenirs that I sent to her in good time. And with that she became a complete stranger in this town, where she will doubtless never set foot again.

"You are a true friend." Everyone knows what that means. A true friend, at two hundred leagues away: but don't cross those two hundred leagues! Come on, it is absolute indifference on her part. Me too, I ought to put myself in unison, seek some other interest in life.

Tomorrow I will apply for a hunting license.

September 1, 1873.

I made an attempt.

Poorly trained dog. All the partridges that I saw flew too far away. I missed a rabbit. On return, I discharged my two shots at the swallows, in flight. I killed one of them. My lead shot touched its heart. It has got a belly and neck covered with pretty white feathers. I just took it in hand. Its little body is still warm.

September 10.

I'm packing my trunks. In three quarters of an hour, the omnibus of the local train is coming to fetch them, and I depart. I feel completely light and at ease.

The express train for Paris! The same one that Helen took one evening, five years ago.

Chapter 9

Paris, September 21.

I leave her place. I saw her. I spent the afternoon with her.

It was two o'clock. Having eaten lunch at my hotel, I took a *mazagran* at the café Riche. Since I came to Paris, I was putting off my visit to see Helen, day after day. Then suddenly:

"Waiter, something to write with!"

And I wrote on one of my cards:

"My dear Helen,

"Here for ten days. Would you like to meet? Tomorrow, I will stop by your place, around three o'clock. – Your old friend."

Then, I put my card in an envelope and, paying for my drink, I asked for a porter. All of the sudden, I called the waiter back again:

"No! no porter!"

And I left the café. On the boulevard, undecided, I walked for a while, letter in hand. What was I going to do for the next twenty-four hours? Waiting would gnaw at me with impatience. Wouldn't it be better just to get it over with? I've been desirous of this moment for five years now: to see Helen once again had become my obsession. A gentle autumn sun livened up the sidewalk, embellished the women, cheered up the strollers. My indecision ceased, I tore up the letter.

"I will see her!"

I took the rue de la Chaussée-d'Antin. However, I entered a tobacco shop, where I chose a very expensive Claro cigar. At Place de la Trinité, I stopped and looked at the square for a moment. Children played on the gravel paths, both in the shade of the branches, and in the sun. Around them, birds flew on the freshly watered lawn. Young mothers, the same age as Helen, sitting in their rustic armchairs, chatted, embroidered. Then I sat down and smoked for a moment in the square, on a chair. The woman renting the chairs appeared, holding out a small ticket to me. While I gave her my two *sous*, what temptations I had to speak with her about Helen, to describe her to her, to ask her if a lady like this or like that didn't come here sometimes with a little girl! No! she probably never stopped here, Helen, in this miniscule square, which was elegant, but of a working-class woman's elegance, good for the brats of the quarter's shopkeeper to play in. Did she often visit Monceaux Park? The garden of the Tuileries? The Bois de Bologne? What fortunate and charming corner of Paris did she like best, to visit each day, to read, to work, to dream? What was her existence like these last five years, since the morning she wrote to me, "I'm in love for the first time in my life." I knew nothing and, in a position now to learn everything in several minutes, there I was suddenly, nailed to my chair, hesitant and apprehensive, like a man who no longer dares to unseal the letter that will decide the rest of his life for him. Finally my cigar went out. Three o'clock sounded.

"Let's go... Any later and I would find she'd gone out."

I immediately climbed rue de Londres. Place de l'Europe. A locomotive's whistle! I was already in rue de Saint-Pétersbourg, on the right-hand sidewalk. I raised my eyes: "No. 16..." It was 16 *bis*, next door, an extremely beautiful house of new Paris in the style of Mr. Haussmann. My ringing of the bell resounded profoundly in my chest. The concierge was in front of the *loge*.

"Mrs...?"

It burned my mouth to pronounce the name. I overcame my repugnance.

"Mrs. de Vandeuilles?"

"Fourth floor above the mezzanine, door on the right."

The stairway, superb, easy to climb, covered with carpet from step to step. At each floor, to the right of the window, a large seat covered in velvet. I sat on the third floor, to try and overcome my heart's beating. Then, climbing very quickly the last steps, I rang. A maid. I gave her my card.

"I will see, sir..."

And, having introduced me into the salon, she closed the door on me. I was obliged once again to sit down. But I felt happy. There was something of Helen in the atmosphere. Something of her in the taste and harmony of the furnishing in the room, in the arrangement of certain objects, in the abandon of certain others. I had already seen somewhere drapes like these: yes, before, in her room as a young girl. And that large Russian, leather-bound album with the silver corners and clasp, I had given it to her. I began to leaf through it. At the back, several new photographs: but the old ones were still there, in the same order. At the front of it, Major Derval, with his ribbon, his fierce attitude. Then me, ten years younger. Then Helen, in divers poses, at different epochs: Helen as a child, in short dresses; Helen taking first communion; Helen in her school uniform at Saint-Denis; Helen as a young woman; Helen married. Finally a recent photograph that I didn't recognize: Helen in Paris, more beautiful and more desirable than ever, always proud, more like a woman. I contemplated her avidly, when the door opened. It was her! With a child on her arm!

I got up quickly. And pressed her free hand. She disengaged it slowly, and, presenting me to her daughter:

"Look at her... What do you think? Her name is Lucienne..."

But she didn't tell me to embrace her. I read her thoughts in her eyes: Lucienne, it was her fault! She didn't hide it: she adored her, she was very proud of her. But an exquisite tactfulness forbade Helen to push her into my arms. Only, at the very thought of the exceptional situation forced on this little being, she lowered her long eyelashes as she gazed at her. She smothered her with a look of commiseration and tenderness, then she began to kiss her crazily, in order to compensate her for others' injustice. Then, while Helen got carried way with maternal affection, I rediscovered my Helen completely, while she exhibited an immense amount of rebellion: "No one else but me can love my daughter, just me alone!"

As in the past, at that moment, I wanted to surround her with gentleness. I escorted her to the arm chair that I had just quit. Me, one knee on the floor next to the arm chair, I began to play timidly with Lucienne. At first, I took her little hands delicately and, after having touched them to my lips, I let her give me pats on the face. Then, as the child smiled, I exclaimed: "I don't frighten you! Come then, we will be great friends..." And I attracted her to me carefully, from the arms of Helen who didn't dare refuse me. Now, with both knees on the rug, I made the little one burst out laughing, feigning to throw her into the air, above my head, then, suddenly, letting her fall; and, each time, I took advantage of her joy to kiss her furtively on the face, on the neck, on her fine nascent hair. Ah! if any one of my serious colleagues from the Court of Appeals in X*** had been able to see me now! Only, Mr. de Vandeuilles could have entered! A fear of looking ridiculous made me brusquely look at Helen.

"It's how I threw you in the air, like that, you, in the past!"

"Yes, I know, you are a good and faithful friend... And, for five years, what things you must have to tell me!"

With her hand, she indicated a seat next to her. When I sat down:

"So! to start with, my father?" she said with emotion.

But Lucienne, seeing that I wasn't paying any more attention to her, began to cry.

"Hold on!" said Helen.

She took her from me, consoled her, kissed her, then rang and had her taken away.

"So, my poor father?..."

We spoke for a long time about her deceased father. She asked me about things she already knew, multiplying her questions, avid for minute details. All the while satisfying her to the best of my abilities, a part of me was distracted, interested only in the joy of being there, wandering with my eyes from the blue flowers of the carpet to the Japanese vases on the mantle, forcing myself to engrave forever in my mind the imprint of the interior of that room, to be able to invoke it all at will and preserve it in my thoughts for when I should be gone. By the open window, a child's cradle and her playthings stood, in the middle of the sun-drenched balcony. The little cries of Lucienne playing with her nanny could be heard from the adjoining room. And it was above all on Helen that I fixed my attention, engraving in my memory the features of her pale face, the contours of her hair, the least folds of her dressing gown which was a little ample in order to hide her new pregnancy, catching sight of the tip of her slipper that hid itself at each moment like a little fearful animal. And, as we spoke, I vibrated with all the emotions that I saw flitter by in the depths of her large black eyes. Her father's illness: I suffered it with her. The burial: a rage shook me as it did her, on account of the malevolent curiosity of the town's people! A tear trembled between her eye lashes at the thought that, since her running off, she hadn't seen the good man again, that she would never see him again: and my heart was breaking with emotion! Finally, she burst out.

"At least, if I made him suffer, are you sure that he forgave me?"

Her chest heaved deeply as she sobbed. At which moment, just as I had done when I began playing with her daughter, I tried to dry the tears of the mother. I took her hands, counting a little on our old familiarity, when she still wore short dresses and came to sit on the lap of her older friend to confide in him some unbounded joy or some great grief. I told her all that I could discover that was tender and consoling. Her father had forgiven her so well that he was thinking to brave the gossip and come and live with her in Paris, with her! She had done right, having been unhappy in X***, to rise above the prejudices, to brave public opinion openly. One lived only once, after all! Who cared about the sots, the envious, the censure of some puritanical salon-goers, the maxims of certain moralistic idiots, the reprobation of hypocrites? Or principles even... Ah! if the magistrates, my colleagues, could have heard me! I told her things that I don't think ordinarily. Morality, logic, society, I would have reduced them all to dust, to have the wherewithal to sand over and render less slippery the dangerous path that Helen had started down.

"What is all that if you're happy!... But you are happy, at least, right?" I asked her.

And, to sound my thoughts completely, Helen's eyes plunged into my own; I took her hands again and was emboldened to kiss them.

"I could not forgive you, my dear Helen, if you were not happy..."

She disengaged her hands immediately and put on a smile.

"But of course, my friend, I am happy... What makes you think I'm not happy?"

The clock struck the half hour. Helen turned her gaze to look at the clock face.

"Fancy that! It's four thirty," she said. "Hold on."

She opened the door to the dining room, to tell the maid that it was time for Lucienne to have her broth.

"Less bread than ordinarily, please!... She has a bit of an upset stomach."

I rose and picked up my hat from off a piece of furniture.

"I'm disturbing you... I'll take my leave."

"No."

And she took the hat out of my hands. She was not going out this afternoon, for Lucienne was not feeling well. She had nothing planned. We had all the time in the world to chat. Mr. de Vandeuilles would not be home until dinner, towards seven thirty. Wait, wasn't this Thursday? Thursdays, he dined at his circle.

"You don't say! he leaves you all alone!"

"With my daughter," she said, very naturally. Then, she changed the topic of conversation: "Have you seen my dining room?"

The dining room was bright and gay, with its large window opening onto the balcony. Sitting on the lap of the maid, Lucienne drank her broth. Birds originally from the Antilles flittered about in a mahogany bird cage. A block of sunlight landing on the polished parquet reflected into a burst of rays, making the pieces of silverware shine on the buffet, an old oak credence. Now that I had seen the dining room, she wanted me to visit the rest of the apartment: their bedroom, Lucienne's room, the kitchen, and another room, barely furnished that one, Mr. de Vandeuilles' "office." Nothing but a writing desk, four chairs; but no library, not a single book. Fencing foils hung on the wall, with fencing gloves and a fencing mask. A box of pistols on a chair. Helen picked up something that was left on the floor: a case for opera glasses, which she put on the small table by the shelf above the fireplace. Visitor cards, unsealed letters, old admission tickets to weigh-ins, a pipe, and cigarettes... all made a little mess on the mantel.

"He spends almost no time in his office," explained Helen. "Also, he's planning to give me this room soon, when I have need of it."

And she drew her dressing gown more tightly around her pregnant belly.

We had returned to the salon. Instead of sitting down again, she went out onto the balcony, and I followed her. Very spacious, because one could have put a table there and dined, this balcony extended all the way around the apartment. A row of vases, chosen by Helen, arranged along the bannister, gave full display of the gaiety of their flowers, a multicolored array of vivid colors.

"And this view!" cried out Helen, with her elbows on the balcony. "What do you think of this view?"

A vista of the entire European Quarter: tall houses of modern construction, all alike, with superb facades, an entire fanout of wide, evenly laid-out roads, each named after a European capital city. Here and there, the back of a facade, from top to bottom cut out by the groove of a narrow interior courtyard, pierced by a checkerboard of small windows. Sometimes, the glass of a window set on fire, burning red, with the reflection of the setting sun; the stretch of a wall covered by the giant letters of an advertisement. Then, below, directly in front of us, the gaping hole of the railroad; the dark profile of a cast iron bridge, solid and light; a jumble of rails running at the bottom of a waterless channel, where the locomotives came and went, starting off in blueish obscurity. The ones that were leaving began mathematically to move, with the hiccoughs of powerful beats. The others, returning slowing, weary possibly, then disgorging all their vapor at once with a formidable sigh of relief. And the clouds of black smoke escaping out from under the arches of the bridge, unfurling in enlarging rings, dissipating into vapor. Here and there, between the closely positioned telegraph wires, interminable trains maneuvered, jerking on their hubs for long intervals of time. The signals inverted, from time to time, their red and green disks. And all that lay before them was alive, in a prodigiously intense way, – regular, imposing, and grandiose. One felt small before this completely modern spectacle of a force of nature dominated by a highly-efficient, collective, multiplied effort.

"I never really looked at the railroad before!" I exclaimed. "I didn't know it was so beautiful!

"My impression was the same, the first time..."

And this was what made them decide to lodge on the fifth floor. But after a while the eye grew accustomed to the most beautiful things; in the end, it no longer paid attention, except in the evening. It was arresting, once night fell, when the infinity of immobile gas lamps floated above the black lake at the bottom of which the wagons and locomotives continually glided. Lucienne, by this time, was sleeping in her little bed. Helen often came to sit on the balcony, alone, and passed the hours looking out at all the animated lights. There were green lights, red lights, blue lights, which seemed to enjoy pursuing and overpassing one another, like stars from roman candles, while others didn't move at all. The locomotives circulated, superb, all black, in the middle of the redness of their furnaces, puffing, blowing their smoke, ablaze. But I was no longer listening to Helen. I was only thinking about one thing: Mr. de Vandeuilles leaves her alone, and for entire evenings! What other business can he have to keep him company! Helen spoke of a circle: he gambles! Would he spend his evenings visiting the theaters? Did he have other mistresses? Moreau, himself, never went out in the evening, but slept and snored. Was this one better?

"Hello?" she said with a derisive smile, "what are you thinking about?"

And when I did not answer, she added:

"I don't like your distractedness."

She divined my thoughts maybe! My confusion was immense. I tried to tell her timidly:

"When you spend your evenings alone, I would like to be here with you, on this balcony..."

But she cut me off completely, both my arms and legs, with this statement:

"You are still the same, then, my poor Mr. Mure?... Still living on the moon!"

Having returned to the salon, we sat down without saying a word. Head lowered, absorbed, mechanically contemplating the flowers in the rug, I thought: "It is she who's still the same! I know her only too well!... And me, I am nothing to her, I don't count in her life... If she saw me at first willingly, if she made me take a tour of her apartment, it was only to show me the life that she wants everyone, down there in X***, to know about, – that she has all the external trappings of happiness. But when I wanted to dig deeper, after she had tried to change the subject, she rebelled; the interest that I have in her exasperates her, and my pity horrifies her!" All these thoughts and reflections came at me at once, in less time than it takes for me to write about them, painful to carry, like an armful of nettles; then in the middle of these thoughts, this conviction: "She is not happy!" And, at the very core of my being, without my paying much attention to it, a sort of nasty satisfaction, making my wounds less painful, arose. Noticing my hat nearby, on a chair, I picked it up. And, the silence beginning to weigh, I sought for something to say. But I could not find anything now; I would have preferred to leave.

"By the way," I said finally, "I almost forget the main reason for my visit!... I have something for you."

And, pulling out of my wallet, I gave her a letter, from the purchaser of her house in X***, with a check for half the sum due, and a promissory note for the rest. After several more phrases, on various indifferent subjects, I rose.

"Do you need me to do anything for you?"

"Nothing... thank you."

She didn't keep me any longer.

"And Lucienne! I'd like to say goodbye."

"One moment."

She rang. The maid appeared, but Lucienne, a bit fatigued, had been put to bed. She was sleeping.

"We must not wake her. Helen; kiss her good-bye for me."

"But you're not leaving Paris... When will you return?"

"I don't know... In any case, I'll say farewell now."

She held out her hand to me, which I held for a moment in mine, saying to her with a little solemnity:

"Farewell... Helen, farewell!"

It was over. Not only would I not set foot again in her place, but I would board the train the following morning.

When I got back to my hotel, I rang for the bellboy and asked to settle my account.

Chapter 10

*X***, September, 1874.*

Yet another year without my having so much as touched those sheets of paper that I had deposited in the back of a drawer. In one year, nothing.

I heard no more talk about her in X***. Life continues here, flat and monotonous, grey. Some marry, some die, some are born. Last winter, the first president and the public prosecutor gave many dinners. But the de Lancys, already at the end of their wad, passed six months in Lancy, to economize, so it was said. Mr. Jauffret has his ups and his downs at baccarat. He was said to be on the verge of selling his old chalet back to Moreau; but his bad luck must have already stopped, because he had just hired some workers: the facade is being repainted, and there are signs of all sorts of embellishment. Mrs. Jauffret is ever the unsightly, long thin asparagus. Three new circles have opened on the Avenue. And the curator of waters and forests has just received his reassignment notice, because of his wife's scandalous behavior.

Not one word from her. She didn't even let me know about her delivery. Another girl, or was it a boy? I have no idea. And to think that, each time that I received a letter, before opening it, before even casting my eyes on the return address, I felt a flush of hope; then nothing! That's my year in a nutshell.

Oh! I forgot. On vacation over Easter, Moreau

returned to France. He spent half a day in X***, came to see me. Very calm, very satisfied, he made no allusion to the past. We spoke for an hour, of Algeria, politics. "What does he want from me? To what do I owe his visit?" I asked myself all along. He ended by confiding in me that the position of president of the Chamber would soon be vacant in Algiers. He came to sound me out, to know whether I would support him among my friends at the ministry. Why not? We dined together. I wrote three long letters in his presence. Then night fell, and he left.

Same day.

My domestic, Nanon, knocks at the door to my office.

"Come in."

"Sir, it is a 'letter of mourning.'"

It is... from Paris! I look at the return address. I seem to recognize the handwriting! Isn't that Mr. de Vandeuilles'? I open it.

"Mr...,

Mrs. Helen Moreau, née Derval, has the honor of apprising you of the painful loss of her daughter, Miss Lucienne, dead at the age of two and a half years old.

De profundis."

October 1874.

No response, at the end of one long month, to my long letter written to her after Lucienne's death. Knowing her character, I knew, however, to avoid writing anything that might have offended her.

She must be quite sad now. It would be so easy to send me a few lines.

April 25, 1875.

Three more letters, in eight months, without a response. And from me, who can never forget you, Helen! I don't know what to think.

I write to her again.

May 3.

I'm leaving.

Paris, May 4, 7 o'clock in the morning.

I didn't get any sleep last night on the train. Booked a room at the same hotel as three years ago, near Palais-Royal. The bellhop went to order a bath for me. Then I have a bowl of consommé, get dressed, and, despite the early hour, show up at rue de Saint-Pétersbourg.

Chapter 11

Paris, May 5.

What emotions since my arrival! What disquietudes! I have lived more of my life in twenty-four hours here, than over the course of many years in X***. My entire feverish state of mind can be summed up in this one line: "I do not know what's become of Helen."

Yesterday morning, rue de Saint-Pétersbourg. The door was open and the lodging deserted. I had already climbed several stairs, planning, given the early hour, to present my calling card and ask at what hour of the afternoon I could return. All of a sudden, the woman concierge arriving in the courtyard, with a broom in hand, says to me:

"Where are you going?"

"To Mrs. de Vandeuilles'."

"She no longer lives here... over two years now."

Two years! And she didn't let me know! Over the course of these last two years, how many times, have I not pictured her in her apartments, taking care of her daughter, her flowers, and her birds; or, in the evenings, on her balcony, looking at the railroad!

"Are you sure it's been two years?"

"Yes, this April, I remember... When that gentleman gave notice to quit, his lady had just given birth to a stillborn child, a little boy... Their little girl also was ill."

"And their new address?"

The concierge didn't know anymore. Near the fortifications, at Ternes; maybe Passy or Auteuil, or somewhere else. Her husband, however, should know the address, he had helped the movers. An office hand at the ministry of finance, her husband was. Quick, a fiacre, to the ministry! After the office hand had been interrogated, soon I found myself at the entrance of the Cité-des-Fleurs, in the Batignolles. I dismissed the carriage. It was nearly ten o'clock in the morning.

I was not familiar with the Cité-des-Fleurs. At the very end of avenue de Clichy, farther than the last station of the Odéon omnibus, at the end of an eccentric and popular quarter, imagine my surprise! Paris is full of these dazzling surprises. It felt as if I had suddenly stepped into aromatic bosquet that was a bird sanctuary: nothing but greenery, flowers, sunlight, birds flitting about on the tender green lawns. It was all one single garden, made up of two hundred little contiguous gardens separated by low-standing walls hidden under very long climbing plants that were stitched together between two rows of small, pretty town houses. In the middle of it all, between the garden railings, a narrow paved passage, with round-abouts located at intervals. And the deeper I entered into it, the more the sweetness of the spring morning, the suave emanations, the chirpings and sound of wings, spoke to me of Helen. "Behold all that she loves! She has passed by here, I can feel it; she is still here. At the other end, the second-to-last of these gardens on the left, I'm sure it! Perhaps I would not need to ring: between the bars of the railings, I might see her all of a sudden, sitting in the small garden, in a straw hat! All that was needed was for me to find her in black, still in mourning. She wouldn't have wanted to leave these flowers and birds, the last things on earth that Lucienne might have reached her little hands out for..." At the second-to-last house on the left, I look through the railing: no sign of Helen in a straw hat! The garden, larger than the others, is mediocrely maintained. On the door, two or three signs hanging: *family-run pension, – furnished and unfurnished rooms*. I ring the bell, just in case. The maid who comes to answer the door: "I don't know any Mrs. de Vandeuilles, I've only been here three months... I will ask the lady of the house..." But the lady of the house, doubtless at her toilette, makes me wait for a quarter of an hour or more. Through an open window on the ground floor, I can see the eating room where two men lay the tablecloth for the next meal, a skimpy bed-and-breakfast tablecloth with wine stains on it in places. No! Helen would never have stayed here! Finally, the lady of the house arrives, a shapeless mass, overflowing with flesh, a large fifty-year-old gossip, with her hair in ringlets, affable, expansive, completely disposed to chatting.

"Yes, Mrs. de Vandeuilles stayed here..."

My face must have expressed my astonishment.

"One moment, sir, you should know..."

No way to fit a word in edgewise, I had to endure those interminable explications. At first she maintained a bourgeois pension, yes, she, and what a pension! It was not, at least, a townhouse like one of those advertised by the yellow sign I must have seen, at the other end of the Cité, while coming here from avenue de Clichy! That *Cité-des-Fleurs Townhouse*, to be clear, questionably inhabited, dishonored the Cité, "so tranquil, so aristocratic a place, as it should be," whereas *her* pension made no blemish on the place. And her house this, and her house that! And nothing but distinguished persons: retired shopkeepers, pensioned officers, an old noble woman with her son employed at the ministry; all serious people, with good salaries, happy to find gardens in the middle of Paris, a little terrestrial paradise, with the pure air of the countryside. Only, given it was very difficult to choose among boarders, and as she turned away applicants daily, she had some vacant rooms, and was looking to sublet the two unfurnished apartments on the second floor.

"Fancy that! Mrs. de Vandeuilles occupied that room in front... those three windows there..."

The three windows were at this very moment full of sunlight, wide open. In one of them, on a string drawn across it, children's laundry was drying that had just been washed, small socks, little white shirts. And those little socks were no longer Lucienne's.

"Would you be so kind as to let me know their new address..."

"Alas! With all my heart, sir, if I could..."

"What? You don't know it!" I exclaimed, in a panic.

And she, again:

"One moment, sir! I will explain..."

And, to each of my expressions of impatience, when I wanted to cut her short, to spare myself some of her chattering, this stout woman, eternally responded:

"One moment, sir! You must know..."

To begin with, high praise for Helen. She seemed so well bred, so great a lady, and at the same time so polite and sweet. He too was quite distinguished, but more abrupt, more stiff, almost cruel with respect to the poorer folk. Nevertheless, quite an interesting couple the two of them. Now, were they married? were they not? My Goodness! people's affairs are their own business! and one mustn't be sticking one's nose into other people's business, especially when it is a question of honorable folk, keeping their commitments and not attracting unwanted attention to the house: on the contrary! From the beginning of their eighteen-month stay, that young lady appeared to be experiencing some setbacks. The health of her little girl was so delicate. She had decided to live in the house doubtless because the good air of the Cité would do her little one some good, but the little one didn't improve much. And, to tell the truth, the gentleman, he didn't always lead the most regular lifestyle. Like the other boarders, he had his master key to the gate and front door; each night, in spite of the precautions he took to tread stealthily like a thief, everyone heard him come home at ungodly hours. At four o'clock, at five o'clock in the morning! So that the boarders nicknamed him the "baker" because, they said, laughing, Mr. de Vandeuilles had to work through the night, and, like bakers' assistants, he didn't return home until dawn! But, if the boarders laughed, that young lady's eyes were often red.

"He was gambling, right?"

"Hold on, sir, I'll tell you..."

I had heard more than enough. While this woman unwound for me her complaisant explanations, a distressing drama rose up before me. I was putting it all together, now. I divined what had been going on on rue de Saint-Pétersbourg. Then, at the time that Helen was giving premature birth to her stillborn son, Mr. de Vandeuilles was experiencing some large gambling losses. Perhaps the debacle, for a long time imminent, had come to a head right when the counterblow of the father's vice could have been fatal for the about-to-be-born son. In any case, he must have had to produce at all costs some large sums of money, to pay off his debts, and thinking to reduce his expenses, he let go of most of the domestics. Then, having quit the apartment costing two thousand francs a month, Helen had sought preferably something in a distant quarter; then, falling in love at first sight with the Cité-des-Fleurs, not wishing to live anywhere else but here, the only vacancy she could find was the small apartment costing six hundred francs a month. And concern for her daughter's health, and hope that her lover, far from the gambling circles, would change his lifestyle, had gained the upper hand over her personal repugnance to living above a "family pension." But, then, disappointment after disappointment: Lucienne dies, Mr. de Vandeuilles gambles. With her daughter gone, Helen lets herself be persuaded to let her modest personal fortune be devoured by the gambler who is ever hopeful to win back his losses. From there, financial difficulties. They had to let the maid go, Helen takes a room in the house, but her meals are brought to her. The gambler stays out all night, stays away for forty-eight hours without returning; finally, rupture! And there's Helen, at the start of winter, in a terrible situation: all alone in the world, without any family or friends, ruined, disillusioned. With her character, not daring perhaps to go out anymore, to pass under the curious and sympathetic glances of the other boarders. She probably owes money!

"Wait, sir!... Oh! she didn't owe me much: one month behind the rent, and two or three behind on the food, in sum several hundred francs... I didn't press her for it, me, I was not in a hurry, I trusted her... Besides, that lady possessed the wherewithal to respond, yes! a superb set of furniture: the wardrobe with a mirror alone was worth four times the amount she owed me... She was the one who, one morning in October, had me come up to her room to ask me if I could help her find a furniture merchant to come and appraise it. She wanted to sell everything, to leave immediately, perhaps to take a trip... Me, I told her: 'You're making a mistake, Mrs.; you should at least keep a room of your own here; this house is very decent for a woman all alone in the world.' Then, when

I realized that it was pointless to try reasoning with her: 'Alright, just a moment, I need to go into Paris this morning before lunch, I will inform my upholsterer...' In the afternoon, the upholsterer arrived, appraised her furniture at three thousand two hundred francs, she wanted five thousand for them, they settled at four. She got the money the following day, in the morning, spent the day packing her trunks, dined, then my maid went to find her a covered fiacre, at La Fourche station, and that lady departed. For what she owed me, we had come to an agreement; I had her wardrobe with the mirror. What can I say, sir? that wardrobe with the mirror had always caught my eye and now it is standing in my bedroom..."

I was overwhelmed. Helen, departed since October, with four thousand francs, a wreck of a fortune, without saying where she was headed. And it was May now!

"Finally, Madam., try to recall... If Mrs. de Vandeuilles had said anything; is there nothing you can remember, not a trace?... Do you remember her saying anything?"

"One moment, sir..."

And I watched the portly woman make an effort to think. She shook her head, and her two ringlets stirred. No! several days later, the maid who had gone to find the carriage claimed to have seen her again, one evening, on avenue de Clichy. But that was not possible. That maid, having since returned to her home town, must have been mistaken. She herself, not going out but very infrequently in fact, had never run into her boarder since, on the avenue nor any-where else. In her mind, the young lady seemed afraid of winter and loved the sun, must have left for the Midi, perhaps Nice... Seeing that I would not get much more out of her, and wracked by worry, I had already turned my back on her and was moving auto-matically towards the railing, thinking, as I was go-ing, that I would write that very day to one of my fel-low law students of old, a deputy judge in Nice. The large woman, now silent, followed me. Hand on the brass knob, I turned around all of a sudden to thank her and take my leave. It was midday. In front of me, in the dining room, by the open window, some board-ers were already sitting at the table; they looked at us. Then, smiling, while her ringlets swayed gracefully, she said:

"Hold on, sir!... Wouldn't you like to dine with us?"

Eat there, no! But, whatever comes of my ef-forts to find Helen, I will never leave Paris without returning there once more, to the Cité-des-Fleurs.

May 10.

Nothing!

My initiatives at the prefecture, ineffectual. I had her inquired into, at the bureau of furnished ac-commodations, under the different names that I had indicated: Derval..., Vandeuilles..., Moreau. An agent, put at my disposition by the prefect's secretary, had even gone into various townhouses and furnished houses looking for her. No woman named Helen was inscribed under one of those three names.

Nothing in Nice either. My old fellow student, the deputy judge, had just responded to me. He remembers perfectly "the beautiful Mrs. Moreau," he said; and a women like that does not pass by unnoticed. The investigations he had made, to put his mind at rest, had only confirmed what he was already certain of: for the entire winter, Mrs. Moreau had not stepped foot in Nice, nor Monte Carlo, nor Antibes, nor Cannes, nor any intermediary city along the seashore.

So, where is she? In which direction should I continue my investigations. I am restless and rack my brain from morning to night, in sterile attempts. By force of racking my brain, I imagine all sorts of crazy things. At least, if I could find out the license of the covered fiacre hitched up with the two horses that, one evening in October, had come to pick her up with her trunks at the family pension. I would be able to follow Helen's trace a little bit further. The coachman would have informed me where he had brought her that evening: to a hotel, or to the train station! At the hotel I would have been able to discover the new name she had assumed; the train station would probably have helped me to divine the country she traveled to! But my inquiries made at the Regional Office of Small Vehicles were in vain. Needlessly, I put an ad in the *Petit Journal*, which coachmen read. Is she still in Paris? In France even? According to a character such as her own, proud and determined, extreme resolutions are the most probable. Who knows? a new life in America? An early death in a convent? Something else?

The day before yesterday, I visited the Morgue. From the railings of the sad square that is behind Notre-Dame, on first sight of the building on the left, I was seized in my chest by a great emotion. "What if I find myself before her, stretched out on a slab, naked, her face disfigured by grievous contortions, in the agony of death!" I redoubled my pace, I entered. There was no cadaver. Passersby who entered by curiosity had disappointed expressions on their face; others looked at each other and smiled. I couldn't take my eyes off the clothing of those who were long dead, whose identity remains a mystery, lamentable discards left hanging behind the glass partition. Here and there, women's clothing. What kind of heart could have beat beneath that shoddy frock once upon a time! On whose leg was that flesh-colored stocking, pulled taut, now marked by blood, exciting to see! Also, to what passion had they walked, those little boots now covered in muck after having spent some time in the Seine! Was I really quite so sure that they had not been worn by Helen's small feet?

And, yesterday evening, after dinner... It was too early for me to call it a night, I smoked a cigar on the boulevard. All of a sudden, in front of the café des Princes, I stopped, petrified: a woman, alone at a table, before a half-drunk bock of beer, smiled at me. "Helen!... So, there you are, Helen!" I was mistaken; that women resembled her so much, her traits, her look, her smile, – she had to be Helen, and Helen recognized me, called me, made little signs with her head to me. As I remained standing there, unable to take my eyes off her, at the neighboring tables, other women, also alone, began to call me: "Psttt! Hey! Mr.! Psttt!..." She, rising without finishing her bock, walked resolutely straight towards me, and slipped her slender gloved hand under my arm, totally naturally, as if we had known each other for a very long time. Her waist, more slender and petite, didn't resemble Helen's at all. Besides, she was a girl, quite young, twenty or twenty-two years old. But when we had walked beyond the café a little, at the moment when I was going to disengage my arm, she said something to me, I don't know what, and the timber of her voice captivated me by a singular charm. It was a voice that I had heard before and whose vibration was clear, fresh, a little shrill; it brought me back in time: it was Helen's voice when she was a young girl. And I didn't disengage my arm after all, I let her lead me wherever she wanted me to go; I asked random questions of her, just to make her talk; then, half-closing my eyes, forgetting the meaning of her words so as to savor the music, it seemed to me at moments that instead of climbing that rue du Faubourg-Montmartre, we were promenading together through the prairies at Miramont, twenty years earlier! We slowed our pace beside the tall willows, and against me I pressed the arm of that student of Saint-Denis on vacation, who confided serious things to me. Suddenly it was as if I had been woken from a dream. On rue Notre-Dame-de-Lorette, in front of a door, the young girl was ringing and ringing, telling me all the while, in that voice of hers that resembled Helen's: "I'm short two *louis* to pay for the ticket... Am I right in thinking, my dear, that you will be generous?"

Chapter 12

May 12.

The *Cité-des-Fleurs Townhouse*, room 7. – That's where I write these lines. – Helen, found by the greatest of coincidences, is in room 6.

She has no idea that a mere wall separates us. I just heard her move a chair.

Myself, at moments, I pass my hand over my face. I need to pinch myself to be convinced that I am not dreaming. Yes, I am completely awake! Moreover, here's how it happened.

Very simply. I had promised myself that I would return one day or another to that Cité-des-Fleurs where Helen had lived eighteen months previously, the worst eighteen months of her life. Yesterday, at around ten o'clock in the evening, I was going back to my hotel. I was at the place du Palais-Royal. It was a spring night. The place was full of people hanging about enjoying themselves. Couples whispered to each other. For the first time this year, the cafés had placed their tables outside. I entered the tobacco shop de la Civette to have my cigar lit again. Then, as I was standing on the sidewalk, oppressed for finding myself alone on that warm evening, in no hurry to retire for the evening and sure that I could not fall asleep, here's that omnibus with its two red lights approaching: *Odéon-Batignolles-Clichy.* It stopped in front of me. "Fancy that! the same one that goes to Cité-des-Fleurs!" And hardly anyone was on the upper deck. After twenty-five minutes, the omnibus stopped before the last station. I descended from the upper deck, got off, and crossed through the gate of the Cité. A wonderful scent of jasmines, roses, and syringas! An adorable gust of nocturnal emanations, a velvety atmosphere, the palpitating noises of leaves! There, I strolled for a long while among all those gardens, merely adding to the shadows. No moonlight. Nothing but stars and, here and there, above the foliage, two or three windows lit up, making their small yellow mark in the night. Then, continuing to advance, I could not see their yellow lights anymore, and I found myself lost in a shuddering solitude, deep within some perfumed desert, where, isolated from the rest of the world, it seemed to me however that I wasn't far from Helen. She had breathed here, under similar spring nights, and something of her still remained. That suave freshness, the intoxication of those calming exhalations, I took them for a trace of her passage. And lo and behold I found myself at the lower end of the Cité now, at the railing of the bourgeois house. At the other end of the garden, the silent and locked house slept in the shadows. The three windows on the second floor reposed quietly. And I didn't know what to say anymore, me! but it seemed to me that that gate was about to open one more time and let her pass. That was the least it could do! For the longest time, I waited for her! Finally, once she had come, her arm brushed my own and I felt that I was going to faint amidst the caress of her dress. Then, slowly, I came to, imagining that we were walking together, the two of us, pressed against each other. At intervals, at each roundabout in the path, we didn't cut to the right: to make it last, we did the half-tour of the circular sidewalk. There was no hurry, and I didn't say a word to her. She could guess what I had on my mind. Then, brusquely... it wasn't a dream any longer! She was right there, several paces away, a tall woman, with an elegant shape, ringing at the gate of the Cité. The guardian must have been asleep, the gate didn't open. Still ringing, she made a movement, turned half-way round towards the loge: then, through the bars, her face appeared to me in the full light of the reflective lantern. I held back a cry. It was Helen. A little changed after three years, still beautiful, but, as a consequence of my concern for her, doubtless, of a strange beauty that I had never seen before. Ultimately, the guardian pulled the cord to open the gate. Letting the gate close behind her, Helen, very quickly, through the shadows, passed along the sidewalk opposite me, without even looking my way. Almost immediately, she entered the garden on the right, whose gate was standing wide open. She rang again, here, at the *Cité-des-Fleurs Townhouse*. I could not get over my stupefaction when I saw the light in the window of the second floor turn on. Helen was in her room.

Room number 6, a single window looking out onto the gardens, thirty-five francs per month, forty with service. She has been living here for more than six months, in the townhouse, passing for a very decent women, a widow, having come upon hard times. I learned all about it in the morning, having returned at an early hour to rent a room myself. "In fact," responded the porter, "number seven is vacant. Would the gentleman like to see number 7?"

"What floor?"

"The second."

And I remembered having seen Helen's light from the second! We ascended. When I visited the room, admired the view of the gardens, haggled a little on the price for appearance's sake, after having complained about not having name tags on the doors:

"Eh! speaking of which, whom would I have for neighbors?"

"Oh! sir, a very quiet person..." And then he began to tell me about her, giving me all sorts of details about "Mrs. Helen" and her withdrawn existence. She made no sound, one could not tell she was in the townhouse, she never received visitors, having her meals brought to her door two times a day, never exiting almost.

"Okay then, that's good, I will take the room and will pay you in advance for the first two weeks."

We go down to the office. He passes the register to me. And I recognized a line of Helen's writing: "Mrs. Helen, widow, née..." In place of Derval, she had written: *Valder*. I wrote my name following hers. And I left to get my trunks. One hour later, I was back. And there I was installed in room number 7, next to Helen.

May 13.

I feel both very sad and very happy at the same time.

For twenty-four hours, living thus in Helen's presence, gives me untold pleasure. She is there, two paces away from me, under my protection. The wall is thin. If she opens her window, if she walks, if she coughs, I hear her. Last evening, toward midnight, when she had gone to bed, the bedspring creaked. And this morning, Philippe, the porter, whom I rang for, not coming, I opened the door a crack: before her door I saw her small boots, her pretty little ankle boots made of the same leather used to make hand gloves. My faith! I couldn't help myself, I had to go and touch them. I almost kissed them, all covered with mud from the day before.

As much to say that it rained yesterday evening: a frightful rain, beating on the window panes so strongly that my new room had soon been transformed into a small lake. In spite of the weather, she left her room after dinner, around eight thirty in the evening. Philippe, whom I immediately rang for with the pretext of getting rid of the water, informed me that Mrs. Helen always left like that after her dinner; every evening, regardless of the weather, and didn't return until eleven o'clock.

"Has she been in that habit for a long time?"

"No, sir; only for the last three weeks."

"Ah!" I said with feigned indifference. And I began to speak with him about something else. Then, suddenly, point-blank, I asked him: "Where the devil do you think she's going in this weather, that neighbor of mine?" Then, with his hands brought close together, the coarse individual began to make an obscene gesture. And he laughed coarsely, loudly. I would have slapped him. But I restrained myself. "Come now!" I said coldly, "You don't really think so?" Without saying another word, Philippe continued laughing, with that coarse laugh of his that seemed to sully Helen. Then, seeing my face in a knot, he stammered some explanations. He said it like that, he said, without really knowing. The lady was by all appearances honest. And he recognized honest people, that man, who for thirty years now had worked in furnished townhouses!

"Only, when I had seen her for the first time, that lady, I knew I had seen something new. A true bit of royalty!" Kidding around is kidding around, but that did not prevent him from calling a spade a spade. At that moment, right next to my room, in the hallway, we heard a key open her door.

"Huh!" cried Philippe surprised, "she's back already?"

It was not ten o'clock.

"The rain must have forced her to return."

Suddenly, bringing his hands to his face:

"And I haven't brought up her towels, nor her carafe!"

He left me, running downstairs.

So Helen went outside every day at the same hour: I must find out where she goes. This evening, I will follow her.

Same day, six o'clock in the evening.

She's eating dinner. I hear the sound of a fork against a plate... For seven months now, morning and evening, she takes her meals like this in her room, alone... She pours herself something to drink... What a life! Not a hand to hold, not an ear to receive a secret. What must be going on in her head? The inclement weather and her isolation must make the time pass slowly for her! Who knows whether she regrets anything from her past, whether she thinks sometimes of X***, of those who envied her distinction and her beauty, of her father whom she never saw again, of me?... Had she ever been on the verge of writing to me? There, she's finished her meal. Philippe, whom she rang for, takes away her setting.

Seven o'clock.

She just opened her window. Through a small hole made by a pin prick in my curtain, I saw a little bit of her hair. Resting on her elbows, she looks out over the Cité-des-Fleurs. It's no longer raining. A beautiful end to a spring day. Her lungs breathe in the scented air that rises from these gardens. Certain corners of the greenery recede and deepen with a bluish gentleness, while the rooves of the small townhouses opposite hers stand out, yellow in the setting sun. All sorts of birds sing simultaneously. She no longer possesses birds from the Antilles. The mahogany birdcage is gone as with the rest of her things... Four thousand francs! Seven months' later and all she had left were four thousand francs! How many months, until that sum is finished, can she continue to live? Maybe another seven months? Maybe a year? Who knows! until next spring and then? Does she take these realities into consideration sometimes? After a while, I asked myself what she was doing there at the window, whence I heard a certain imperceptible sound, a sort of muted grinding: she was filing her nails! Before beginning to get dressed, she filed her nails!

Eight o'clock.

She's ready. Her toilette is doubtless finished. The door of an armoire with a mirror just opened and closed. I believe that she is standing up, about to put her hat on and looking at herself in the mirror. Does she attempt to use cosmetics sometimes to darken her first white hairs? Has she discovered a precocious wrinkle in her face? She is thirty-six years old today plus two or three months. Not old, but not completely young either. And this must be a great sadness for a woman to admit: "youth passes." What's more, beauty is made only of adolescence and freshness. And, as poorly as I made her out the other evening, she surprised me by a novelty of beauty, a touching and wounded expression. Her eyes which were rattled, but enlarged and deeper, burned in the night with I don't know what mysterious, disquieting flame... Why did she just grab a chair and sit down?

Eight thirty.

What's going on? For over a quarter of an hour while

she's sitting down, I can hear nothing. What is she doing? What is she thinking about? What is she waiting for? Yesterday, by this time, she had already departed. Now, perhaps it is me who is too impatient. My heart beats. I'm so troubled, it is as if I was about to commit some base action. Do I really have the right to follow her, to spy on her like this, to discover her secret? I'm doing it for her, what's best for her only. But aren't I doing it also for myself? Never mind! For me and for her, right or wrong, I'm feverish: why doesn't she hurry up! On the other hand, maybe she has no secret at all.

Nine o'clock.

She has paced up and down her room for some time now, like someone who is reflecting and does not know what decision to make. Then I can't hear her anymore. I believe she has sat down again. It's getting late. The hands on the clock continue to move! Now, whether she departs or not, I don't care. My fever has abated. I have only sadness and discouragement. What am I doing here, me, Mr. Mure, a judge, a serious man, nearly fifty years old? My ear pressed up against a wall, like a jealous husband! This spying like a policeman in a rundown furnished townhouse, is it appropriate for my age, for my social station? Is it appropriate for my baldness and my white hairs? Nobody at X*** would believe it! The Palace of Justice, my colleagues, with a telescope, if they could see me here and follow my improbable adventure: what outbursts of laughter! They'd be laughing uncontrollably for several months, in the reading room, at the circle! And at the Jauffret's? And at the Thursday night soirées at Mrs. de Lancy's? But there, I'm not the one they'd tear apart the most! If they knew that the poor Helen was here, and if they saw this townhouse! Who would defend her in that provincial, hypocritical, and straight-laced society? Nobody would think to be fair, to take into account the circumstances of her fall. Nobody would admire her pride to a fault, her courage to go to the extremity, her contempt for money, which has been her ruin, the simple grandeur of her resignation to accept all consequences. Not one of them would appreciate the feeling that prevented her from distancing herself from the Cité-des-Fleurs, where the memory of her daughter and something of her lost illusions must linger for her in this charming corner of Paris. They would only wish to see the shady aspect of the furnished house, the ugly yellow writing on the door, the mud poorly swept up on the stairway. And the furnishings? Philippe told me that Mrs. Helen's and my rooms were the "best of the house." Here, on the bed and at the window, dirty blue damask curtains. The dreadful grimace of luxury, shabby mahogany, torn wallpaper. Above all that ignoble settee, dusty and oily, worn out by vice.

Ten o'clock.

She does not go out. Her door is locked fast. I hear her undressing. She's going to sleep for the night, there, next to me: I forget the rest. And I'm going to be happy.

Chapter 13

Night from May 13 to 14... eleven o'clock in the evening.

Nothing! She didn't return!

I can't believe my eyes. I lost sight of her at the end of avenue de Saint-Ouen. Poor Helen!

I'll exit again.

Midnight.

Again, nothing! I walked in vain throughout the quarter unable to find her. I will go and wait for her at the window.

One o'clock.

The Cité-des-Fleurs sleeps. A dark night. Nothing lit but the guardian's lantern. From the moment she rings at the gate, in the little yellow light of the reflector, I will recognize her. But, for a long time now, nobody rings. A great silence. In the room, the tick-tock of the pendulum. In the distance, somewhere in the night, the breathing of the colossus of Paris that relaxes. A moist breeze, blowing in my face, drove two or three large water drops into my eyes. But I'm not crying. Something strangles me, a weight prevents me from breathing, sometimes a shiver seizes me completely, while my face burns. I take up my place again at the window.

Two o'clock.

Now, she will not come back. What can I do to shorten the hours until day?

Write? Here's what I came up with:

This evening, she dined very quickly. Philippe not having come up again in order to take away her dishes, – two or three impatient, imperious rings of the bell. Then, suddenly, instead of resting on her elbows at the window, she got dressed. But she took forever to get dressed. Ready towards eight o'clock, she exited.

It wasn't night yet. Even though she's a little short-sighted, I followed her at a distance, prepared to hide my face, to turn aside, if she should turn around.

She walked slowly up the avenue de Clichy, on the left-hand sidewalk, as slowly as the omnibus from Odéon in the middle of the pavement, a little ahead of her, climbing up the hill of La Fourche with a backup horse pulling. Tall, slender, very simply dressed. Her black dress added however a touch of elegance and aristocracy amidst of the banality of the passersby: employees, workers in overalls, shop girls returning from the interior of Paris. Here and there, heads turned to look at her. When she had passed a large café at the end of which a gas lamp was already lit, a waiter exited, walked out into the middle of the sidewalk, and watched her as she distanced herself.

In a moment's time, I lost sight of her: she had entered a boutique. A florist's shop, whose green and odorous display window lent an aspect of spring between the pork butcher and the wine merchant. She came out again with a small bouquet of violets.

At La Fourche, leaving behind the backup horse and its guide, the omnibus left at a trot towards the interior of Paris. She stopped for a minute, turned towards avenue de Saint-Ouen, finding interest perhaps in the interminable double row of gas lamps, lit up in the twilight, thrusting their golden points of light into the suburb. Was she waiting for someone before exiting from one of those first houses, which were ugly and base? She looked farther away also, there where the avenue grew more vulgar still, until it turned into the quarter of rag-and-bone men near the barrier. Seeing nothing coming, she continued to mount the avenue de Clichy. Already at the top of it, the omnibus disappeared behind Marshal Moncey's monument.

As far up as with the small dance hall, as she had just passed over to the sidewalk on the right, suddenly, just above her head almost, the letters "*Bal du Chalet*" were lit up in small flames. She had to make a brusk detour: two guttersnipes in soft caps burst out of the dance hall, nearly fell on her, pretending to box. Helen never turned back; but she hastened her pace until she reached the restaurant *Père Lathuile.*

Now she was at place Moncey, in front of the Marshal leaning on his canon, defending the ancient barrier in an artificial pose of heroism. Bathed in a bluish twilight, the place seemed larger. To the left, the boulevard de Clichy, to the right, the boulevard des Batignolles, both proceeded, very wide, giving the idea of an endless belt encircling Paris. In front, the contiguous facades of two cafés, all ablaze at the entrance of rue de Clichy, which descends towards the heart of the city. Helen, at the end of the sidewalk, stopped, seemed indecisive. What was she going to do? Cross the place, enter into an omnibus station, ask for one of those fiacres that were waiting in a line, with their red, green, yellow lanterns lit up? Perhaps continue along the exterior boulevards, promenading without purpose? Perhaps return immediately, not having the courage to go any farther, and go home?

A shrill street organ could be heard in the middle of the boulevard des Batignolles. From a little neighboring café-concert, ensconced on the first floor of a shady, furnished townhouse, languorous baritone roulades, wailing love, arrived, accompanied by a piano. Next to the tobacco-grocery shop, a greasy spoon, where people were seen dining at tables without tablecloths, and which emitted an odor of frying oil. In front of the journal merchant's kiosk, a girl without a hat on, her small dog under one arm, bought a journal for one *sou*. Men, vaguely drunk, grazed along the houses with a staggering pace. And Helen hesitated, always at the same spot, smelling her violets for a long time.

She ended up by turning to the right, avoided a Wallace fountain where kids amused themselves, splashing each other with full cups of water, and took the exterior boulevard. The street organ continued to play. Everyone was attracted by its persistent and nasal sound, whose wheezing through air vents, from time to time, reminded one of an asthmatic clown. Already a large circle of people occupied all the wide sidewalk, from one row of the small plane trees to the other. In the middle of them, a street entertainer, wearing a long black jacket, under which his undershirt could be seen, stretched out on an old rug, lighting and arranging in a circle six candles, stuck into the neck of bottles. Enormous weights had been deposited at the foot of a tree. There, a second street entertainer, also in a jacket, waited, sitting on a barrel, his legs swinging.

Heads were drawn to him with a curiosity, and certain people in the crowd got out of line. And, from mouth to mouth, a name circulated: "Fernand!... Fernand!" They were his regular nightly audience, the people of the quarter, coming each day to the same place to see Fernand work: shopkeepers from across the street without hats on, cooks in their aprons, workers returning home with their tools, couples gone outside to breathe the air along the exterior boulevard. And the girl without a hat on who had just bought a journal was there, her dog under one arm, back a ways, trying to the right and to the left to see, with a smile on her face. While in the front row, where they had edged forward while pushing aside the others, five or six shameless girls from twelve to fourteen years old, looking like they had just gotten out of bed, with their dresses trussed up like slatterns, devoured with their eyes the legs of the street performer wearing a flesh-colored undershirt and saying what they thought out loud: "Fernand has something, this evening, for sure!"

"Yes, he looks completely bored. Maybe he fell out with his girlfriend!"

"Look at him! Clara, he looks pretty loaded up with the pomade." One of them was emboldened enough to touch the ends of the dark-red velvet ribbon that was pulling back Fernand's thick hair. He raised his head.

"Get back, you pile of vermin!"

And they caught a glimpse of his matte forehead, a little low, his handsome face like that of a medallion, so strong and pure of contour, so completely brown, one might say it was made of bronze. And the crowd stepped back, not just the girls, but the curious too, leaving round him and his barrel a respectful distance.

The street organ called again. Now, it was completely dark outside. The candles, from the top of their bottles, emitted a vacillating, smoky light. And Fernand remained still again as if crushed down under the weight of his shock of black, naturally curly hair. Only the top of his skull could be seen clearly, a little depressed under the fleece of hair made lustrous by the oil, a head of Hercules, with a narrow brain, never able to contain more than one thought at a time. And this thought that he had, at this moment, kept his face down, fastened his absorbed gaze to the earth, while the other street performer, his jacket removed, was making himself hoarse by shouting out his patter which the public didn't listen to. That guy, already old, ugly, and badly shaped, although walking on his hands for a good while, with his two legs crossed behind the nape of his neck, nobody looked at him. Now and then a rare *sou* was thrown onto the rug. Helen's gloved hand passed between two people standing in front of her, and threw a silver coin.

But Fernand was no longer alone as he sat on his barrel. Two guttersnipes wearing caps, probably the same two who were grappling in front of the dance hall earlier, arrived and surrounded him, extending a hand to him. Fernand placed his feet on the ground with a lively gesture. The three of them spoke confidentially, looking into each other's eyes, with little laughs, good buddies who were in on something and understood each other's half words. He had to know the news, and that the business at hand, for sure, was going well. Fernand's beautiful eyes, completely gladdened, sparkled with joy and hope now, reviewing the public who stood before him, until he settled on the place where Helen was hiding in the shadows:

"Thank you! and see you tomorrow!" he said at the top of his voice, while shaking the hand of his two friends.

And with a last look at these two, he added:

"Yes, I will tell you everything that happens..."

Bent down at the foot of the tree where the weights were deposited, Fernand was throwing them already into the middle of the open space lit up by the candles, one by one. There were nine in all. And, with each toss, the ground shook with a loud thump. Now standing up on the old rug, Fernand collected the several *sous* thrown there. The silver coin from Helen made him smile; and his beautiful, almond eyes, shaded by long lashes, glimmered with pleasure, looking around again for Helen. Suddenly, his forehead creased; shrugging his shoulders with affectation, he began to look the public in the face, with a dissatisfied and provocative attitude.

"Quiet!" he said with a gesture to the man who was turning the handle of the street organ.

The organ fell silent. A profound silence ensued.

"Twenty-five, twenty-six, and twenty-seven!" said the street entertainer. "I have counted it well... That only makes twenty-seven sous, ladies and gentlemen... Uh, well, know one thing: I'm not happy!... Do you think that we can live on twenty-seven *sous* per day, my associate and me? He, my associate, whom you have just seen working, ask him if he's more happy than I am... He will tell you he'd find it more pleasant to spend his evening at the wine merchant's quietly drinking his half liter... Isn't that right, old man?"

The "old man" made an energetic "yes" with his head and hands.

"And as for me, ladies," continued Fernand, "who among you says I do not have a female acquaintance?... Some high-society woman?... A duchess maybe with a crush on me?... And who would be quite happy at this very moment to be going, arm in arm with me, to Baratte's to eat a dozen... Ah, well, instead of me dancing in faubourg Saint-Germain, I'm here on the boulevard des Batignolles, hanging out and trying to act clever... Consider me in that light!"

And in the blink of an eye, he had thrown his old jacket away, and he appeared naked, in a flesh-colored undershirt, completely naked, with a tight pair of cherry-red, satin shorts on. A small shiver passed through the crowd.

"If I have to slog away in this costume, it's to make a living..."

And he waited. Five or six *sous* only fell. He picked them up. Then, shaking his head with feigned anger:

"That does not cut it!... I need five francs, not one *sou* less than that! or you will not see me lift the barrel with my teeth... Listen up, five francs! and be quick about it... Today, I don't have time to wait as long as I did yesterday... Let's go, music!"

The street organ played a Waltz now. Rapidly, the two street entertainers lifted the barrel, length-wise, and placed it in the middle of two supports. Then a chair, right on top of the barrel. And, standing on the chair, his arms crossed, calm and sure of his influence over the crowd whose heads only came up to his feet, disdaining even to amuse them with the jugglery of the weights that day, as not needed, Fernand, waited for his five franks.

Every face was looking at him. The brightness

of a streetlight, near his head, made his head of hair look fleecy, made a circle of light around his strong neck, molded his torso, his flat stomach, his large back; while in the dancing light of the candles, what was most handsome about him, his legs, colossal thighs and calves, fine joints, the perfect image of two lively rippling muscles. And looking at him, employees who had renounced the café in order to economize felt sad unconsciously, poor wimpy race that they were. The laborers going back home with their tools said to each other that with his biceps, in their line of work, they would be a boss somewhere, and the envy of their comrades. And the corner grocer, with his bald head and fat stomach, hands in his pockets, calculating approximately what the strapping lad could still do for him, one evening or another. Then, "he's only twenty-four years old!" sighed the cooks. The girl without a hat holding a dog under one arm: "If only he were built like that at least, the guy who gives me a thrashing!" And the bourgeois couples that had gone outside to breathe fresh air, the Mrs. couldn't help making physical comparisons to her husband's disadvantage; while the husband, himself, under his tall hat, rolled around this thought: "There's a fellow who would never get hitched." Even the naughty little fourteen year olds still wet behind the ears, who continued to draw near, the saucy ones, ended up by standing against the barrel, their necks wrenched, in order to see: "What do you think, Clara, if his shorts suddenly split!" And Helen didn't walk away.

However, I didn't see her again, as more people arrived. Each one pushing the other, pressing, wanting to get upfront. But I knew she was still there, staying humble and making herself small, happy to disappear, letting the louts push ahead of her. And my entire soul was caught up in it, with each instant, in that shadow, trying to hide her and protect her, like her long black lowered veil. The street organ played the same air over and over again. It rained *sous* from time to time. Some of them struck the barrel with a little crisp sound, bouncing off. The "old man" collected them around the candles and threw them into a chipped plate at the corner of the unfolded rug. Fernand ended up jumping to the ground. And the "old man" climbed up to take his place on the barrel, sat on the chair, while Fernand counted the money again.

"This time, four francs, three sous! still not the amount I asked for... But I'm in a hurry. I want to lift up the barrel right now. Only, when my teeth are holding it in the air with the weight of that man on top of it, you others, instead of applauding, you will throw me another franc. Glory is a fine thing, but eating?... And don't amuse yourselves by crying: "Enough!" as you normally do. That annoys me... And I won't let the barrel go until I have my one hundred dred *sous*... Thus, your pity won't help: you can only help with your pockets!"

Then, all at once, resolutely, with the sudden decision of a man who had to make an extraordinary effort and who does not want to reflect on it for fear he may lack courage, Fernand, bit into the edge of the barrel. At a familiar location, where the wood had been a bit pared with a knife, and where each of his teeth found their accustomed imprint. Then began a long, interminable minute. Buttressing himself up by his legs, his two hands holding onto his sides, his head dug into his chest, his neck shortened, swollen, ready to burst, Fernand held the barrel in the air, with a man sitting on a chair on top of it, with his arms crossed. And Fernand closed his eyes, his face red, then crimson. And everyone held their breath. The street organ seemed to play from afar, while the rumbling of an omnibus on the pavement crushed the ground and weighed on everyone's chests. Then the *sous* began to rain, left and right, like large water drops falling from an electric storm cloud. In the end, as the public grew tired first, applause, mixed with murmurs, broke out. Fernand, scarlet in the face, sweating all over, he didn't let the barrel down. "Enough! enough!" The crowd rushed toward him and took it away from him. When the barrel rested again on the two supports, everyone sighed with relief. And Fernand, after shaking his head two or three times, right there, on the spot, dazed, took several steps back, like a drunken man, and collapsed on a bench.

The circle broke up. It was over. Only, before going away, many people approached the bench and contemplated the exhausted street performer. There was one last round of applause. "He's sweating! – Beads of sweat on his shorts! – He wouldn't dare do it again! – Why is he hiding his face in a handkerchief! – One would think his teeth hurt, look! – His teeth! All the same, they must be very strong!" Then the lady and gentleman went on their way, arm in arm. The cooks, for fear of a scolding, ran off. The girl without a hat on put her little dog down, left it alone for a moment at the foot of the plane tree, then, at a small distance away, called to it. And the employees pricked up their ears: "Ten o'clock! It's time to go to bed." The shopkeepers across the street could already be heard closing up shop. The gathering was reduced to the mischievous little fourteen-year-old girls and little rascals. Helen was still there, to the side, in the shadows.

Then what happened? I don't know anymore. What I saw was so extraordinary that, even now, I can barely believe my eyes. Suddenly, on the bench, Fernand, having shaken off his state of prostration, raised his head and looked straight at Helen! Helen, through her veil, looked at him also. His eyes gleaming with joy, smiling. He even had the audacity to make a small gesture. But, with lowered head, as if ashamed, Helen had already taken off. Now, with slow steps, she was walking along the exterior boulevard. A little ahead of her, the girl without the hat was holding her dog in her arms again; at the approach of several passersby, she crossed, running, from one plane tree to the other. On the same sidewalk, Helen was waiting for a street performer! No! it was not possible! How I stayed there, me, riveted to the ground, petrified with surprise, an idiot full of consternation! All I had to do was move, go up to her and look at her, dare to speak with her, and I would have clearly seen that it was not Helen! And then, even if it was Helen, I wouldn't have seen anything: no exchanged glances, not a smile, not a gesture. That Fernand would not come! Together with his comrade, he carried the barrel and its supports, the weights, the old rug, the broken plate across the street to a wine merchant's shop!

There at the habitual depository for their equipment, they sure took their time the two of them, relaxing and drinking! Suddenly, as my entire soul was in a state of violent agitation, someone exited the wine merchant's shop, crossed the pavement, passed near me. It was Fernand! Fernand in a fitted black overcoat and a little, round red hat, the "melon" worn by up-scale shop assistants and low-level employees, worn on the back of the head; in all, very proper. Nothing left of the street performer, save the two red boots that rose very high on his legs and, at times, a small piece of a pinkish undershirt, visible under the long overcoat. He was smoking a cigar. He passed by very quickly, a cane in hand, twirling it around. He would have caught up to Helen in no time, who had her back to him, who made no sign whatsoever; only, she redoubled her pace. He didn't even reach for his hat with his hand, and continued smoking. I saw them walking away like that, in parallel, a meter a part, and I asked myself if they weren't speaking with one another. I hoped not. I followed them from a distance, hoping that they would part ways. No! they walked side by side now! Fernand was talking with animation, turning his head to look at her, getting closer to her. And she, always tending to put a distance between them, went off to the right. They ended up by crossing the road, walking up on the sidewalk along the houses; there, Helen, unable to veer away anymore, skimmed along the facades, while Fernand was practically right up against her. At the corner of the boulevard and rue de Rome, Helen turned brusquely, taking an obscure and deserted street. Then, Fernand, throwing away his cigar, passed his arm around her waist. And with his free hand, he held one of Helen's hands. He kissed it in the shadows. Helen let him do it! At that moment my legs, heavy like lead, remained frozen in place. A kind of veil passed before my eyes. A repressed sob was followed by profound tremors in my chest. Helen, this time, was lost, completely lost, and I could do nothing about it, not cry, not weep. I turned my head away. At this moment, a train leaving Paris at full steam would be swallowed up while whistling as it passed under the bridge of the exterior boulevard. And the bridge trembled. Thick smoke sprung up in large flocks from the railing around the parapet, rose up in a cloud. Then the train whistled again, invisible and already distant, from the country-side. On this side of Paris, the cloud of smoke dissi-pated; and as it did, in its escape from the Saint-Lazare train station, I saw an infinity of little, immo-bile, yellow flames appear, floating on the surface of the black lake... It was there, to the left and down a ways, not far: the windows of her old apartment on rue de Saint-Pétersbourg! the balcony where, once, at the fall of day, she had made me admire the railroad! I recognized the tall modern houses with windows in a checkerboard pattern, all lit up at this hour. There, for three years now, other women lived whose exis-tence perhaps had remained the same: easy and soft, occupied by regular feelings, happy in their bourgeois existence; while Helen... My eyes grew moist. All the little yellow lights of the train station disappeared, drowned in my tears. What I was looking distinctly at now was the entire chain of fatalities of Helen's life: Fernand! Mr. de Vandeuilles! Moreau! And, in the beginning, me! Me, first cause of it all! Me, I had found her a husband! Me, I had pushed her into elegant adultery! Me, I had let her slide into the mud! It was then up to me to pick her back up again. At this point, it was merely a matter of duty to follow those two, a rage to catch up to them, to speak with them. But the rue de Rome was deserted. They must have turned to the right, gone back to the Batignolles. I began to run up to the corner of rue des Dames; then, not seeing them, to the corner of rue de La Condamine. On rue Legendre, a couple was walking towards the square. It wasn't them! I climbed back up avenue de Clichy as far as La Fourche. There, it was no mistake, I saw them both again, down below on avenue de Saint-Ouen. They passed under the light of a streetlamp. My far-sighted eyes recognized Helen. But they had too much of a head start. I wandered in vain through a maze of poor, little streets. Then I went home. I looked for her outside my window, then I went out again. Having come back home again, I have just written all this down in an attempt to forget that Helen is now in the arms of Fernand.

Five o'clock in the morning.

Someone rings... The door to the hotel closes again... A light step on the stair... The frou-frou of a silk dress... It's Helen returning, in the early hours of the morning... There she is on the first floor... When she puts her key in the lock, I will be at her feet.

Chapter 14

*X***, November 1878.*

Three and a half years later! Here I am still alone in my apartment, an old bachelor.

Last night's party made me go to bed late. I was agitated. I could barely shut my eyes. But I slept very deeply and it restored me, not waking again until ten o'clock this morning. Barely open, my eyes turned towards the window. A pale winter sun, gay although pale, was beginning to melt the small crystals that were scattered on the outside of the glass panes.

"Fancy that! Last night must have been cold."

And I rang. My old maid, Nanon, who has known me since my birth, entered.

"Good morning, Nanon... Make me a fire."

"Here? in your room?... But the Prussian-style fireplace in your office is already roaring!"

And the rollers in her blinding-white hair seemed to stand on end with surprise.

"Yes, Nanon, in my fireplace..."

"Okay! it appears that you plan to take good care of yourself this winter."

Her entire face, wrinkled and lined with age, smiled maliciously. Then, bending down, in an agile and lively manner, her waist still supple and elegant like that of a young woman, Nanon opened the flue in the fireplace. And, while she was pushing away the old cinders with the shovel, she said:

"Let's see, sir, that important dinner last night? that soirée?... Did everything go according to plan?..."

"Yes, Nanon."

"Lots of important people?"

"Everyone in town."

"Madame de Lancy wore a beautiful dress, I imagine?"

"From Paris!... And from Worth's to boot!... Brought back from their trip to the Exposition."

"And the tall Mrs. Jauffret?... Not too sad for her husband's gambling losses, their chalet sold back to the old proprietor?"

"On the contrary, she's gained weight! But she doesn't have her diamonds anymore."

"And the Marquis de N.N.?... And the wife of the new public prosecutor?... And..."

"You chatterbox, Nanon, can't you hurry it up!"

"There, sir, I've finished... Look at that! I strike the match, it burns like tinder, and you'll be able to get dressed in its warmth, in front of a good little blaze... But I beg you, tell me one thing: Mr. Moreau, your new president, ah, well, what kind of a face did he wear?..."

Then, I got up out of bed. I put on my cotton dressing gown; and, after having shaved my face with warm water, my feet quite warm in my felt slippers, – an excellent purchase which I pat myself on the back for every single day, – I have just eaten breakfast at a corner of the fireplace. Two scrambled eggs with truffles and a cold partridge, young and tender, wrapped in bacon, smelling of mountain thyme. Paired with an excellent wine from the countryside, which in Paris could be marketed as a wine of great distinction. Six years in the bottle with a beautiful yellow tint for aging. The fact is that I've become a gourmand. For dessert, Nanon brought me a mysterious large plate covered by another plate. I lifted the top plate...

"A chestnut gateau! Thank you, my dear maid!"

"You will find it excellent... I didn't skimp on the vanilla, nor the orange blossoms... At least since last winter, I don't remember the recipe any longer!..."

"There's nobody like you, Nanon, nobody!"

"I stuck my fork into the succulent, velvety rich and odoriferous pastry, – Nanon's own secret recipe, which, the day that I lose her, Nanon will bring to the grave with her, – into the succulent pastry covered with a glaze that is white like snow and powdered with blue and pink aniseed. As I took three or four bites from this gateau, I was thinking of my childhood, of the time when I was a gourmand, – like now, – when I knew nothing about life, and when I wore shorts. Then, I folded my napkin, as normal. I drank several small sips of my boiling hot coffee, and I came to sit down, here, in my office. Here, a little tired and desirous of introspection, I opened a drawer that I kept locked, and I took out some papers. The most ancient among them, already yellowed with age. All filled with Helen.

Helen!

Yesterday, the great day, it was important that she be beautiful, and she was. Beautiful! that is to say impressive and gracious, proud and touching, mistress of the house in several places at once for her guests, the heroic queen, magnetizing all the ferocious people in town, which she had recently vanquished and conquered again. She was all that and more! If only old Major Derval could have seen her.

Yesterday. The dinner was scheduled for seven o'clock. But Helen begged me to arrive early, and around five thirty I rang the bell at the chalet.

A red rug in the vestibule. Hangings on the wall, on the ceiling a chandelier ready to be lit, flowers everywhere. The little antechamber on the left transformed into a coatroom, with a large mirror on the back wall, so that the ladies, when removing their coats, could see themselves from head to foot. Myself, I handed over my umbrella together with my overcoat and slipped a ticket with the number 1 on it into my fob.

On the staircase, another rug, more chandeliers, more wall hangings; and, on each step, a double line of rare plants, of natural flowers. Under the gentle warmth emanating from openings in the heater, those flowers filled the air with their perfume. It went to your head like an intoxication. And, in spite of herself, she had thought in advance of the little feet in small satin boots that were going to climb the stairs, light and nervous, shaking with curiosity, envy, and malice.

But a calm, far-sighted, courageous will seemed to have watched over all the preparations. Before asking for anyone, I wanted to cast my eye everywhere. Before leaving the ground floor even, half-opening the door on the right, I looked into the dining room. A domestic was already there lighting the innumerable candles of the candelabra. The table, with eighteen places set, was ready. Around the moss and the flowers strewn in the center of the tablecloth, the eighteen damask table napkins, blinding white, seemed like so many tabernacles each waiting for their devout sacrificer. Large and small glasses, arranged by height, were symmetrically placed, the menu with the name of each guest on each champagne glass. And the transparency of the crystals sparkled, the luminous gleamings of flat dishes troubled you like glances, the flowers burst in extraordinary sonorities of coloration. With the long candles of the candelabra all lit, the entire table, transformed into an ardent chapel, already seemed to burn for some perpetual adoration. Stunned, turning my eyes away, I closed the door.

A glance at the garden through the glass door

of the vestibule. Since the summer evening when Moreau, on the terrace, fell asleep in his armchair, when the journal slipped through his fingers onto the ground, I hadn't walked through those pathways again. Almost nothing had changed! No traces of the Jauffrets' possession, thankfully! I recognized the shape of the clumps of persistent foliage of the copse. By themselves, the four young plane trees on the terrace, unrecognizable after twelve years, having grown into tall trees with enormous trunks, with long branches that never end, now deprived of leaves. After twelve years, so many things! This evening, a party, and, at the same time, winter. The clusters of Venetian lanterns already lit, suspended between each plane tree; the cordons with their colored glass lamps, illuminating the steps of the outdoor stairway, the seats and the pillars on the terrace. But a bitter, glacial, north wind blew at moments, made the small flames lay down all at the same time, extinguished some of them here and there, shook lamentably the great luminous clusters. Suddenly, the paper of one of the Venetian lanterns caught on fire, burned for a second, went out in large, enflamed drops; then, in the middle of that cluster of joyous colors, – a black hole.

I was on the first floor. The vast antechamber, which serves also at the same time as the billiard room, I no longer recognized it. The billiard table had been removed so that people could dance there. A red cloth was draped over the wall-to-wall carpeting; flowers were everywhere, paintings and panoplies, chandeliers. A platform for the orchestra. Then, three reception rooms in a row; in the back, the small blue room. Everything was prepared. The large lamps were already illuminated, their flames kept low. Enormous round logs, thick like tree trunks, burned in the fireplaces. While I presented the tip of my varnished boots near the flame, a door opened and closed at the back of the blue room. I saw Helen's chambermaid enter.

"Good evening, sir!"

She was going to leave.

"Tell me, when does one plan to finish lighting up the rooms?"

"It's not six o'clock yet... the Mrs. has given the order that they be lit at six thirty."

"That's fine."

"The Mrs. will soon be present... Should I tell her now that you are here, sir?"

"No need... Thank you."

I was no longer cold. Distancing myself from the fireplace, I entered the small blue room, that delicious boudoir, which Helen particularly liked. There, nothing had changed. The preparations for the party had not crossed the sill of that sanctuary that was full of Helen and the things that she loved. The intimate lamp, in the accustomed place, emitted its soft light. The new novel with the yellow cover that she was reading, was placed open on the working table. All of a sudden, the back door opened, a naked arm, already decorated with bracelets, a small open hand reached out towards me.

"Helen!"

I had taken her hand and pressed it gently in mine.

"Thank you for being the first to come. As you can see, all the town will be here: I just have to have my dress ironed."

"I'm keeping you... I will let you go."

"Wait."

And, drawing aside the door curtain, she showed herself to me as she was: in white underskirts, a sky-blue corset, her arms and breasts naked, all fresh, all perfumed, and chaste. The contained fever that gave her voice a small shiver, the extraordinary sparkle in her eyes, the animating resolution in her face, adorned her better than any high-necked bodice. And, her face a little lowered in order to show me her coiffure:

"Look... is it okay?"

Then, someone stepped into the adjoining room. Remembering brusquely that she was naked to the waist, she let the curtain close behind her. Me then, standing there, with no time to tell her in a low voice through the tapestry that she looked beautiful and charming. Someone entered. The room valet, on behalf of Moreau, came to tell me:

"The President is at home and asks you, sir, to come upstairs."

"Ah! The President!... Very well! I will go!"

And, on the stairway, while climbing up a floor, "the President" still jarred my senses, like the memory of a shrill, false note vibrating suddenly in the middle of a sweet melody. Not bothering to knock, I turn the knob of the first door; I walk through the antechamber. I find myself in a vast and sumptuous office, with all four walls covered by the books of his library. Ten thousand volumes of law, superbly bound, which had made the trip to and from Africa, I find them all, in the same place, with their spines rigid and all in a row, almost terrible: some red and others black. And an involuntary smile pursed my lips: "The President"! The door of his room was open wide. Standing in front of an oval mirror hanging on the window, already in black pants and varnished boots, a white towel tied behind his neck, Moreau was finishing up shaving.

"Come in, my dear friend... Sit down, but don't say a thing... You could make me cut myself...."

Then, after one instant, wiping carefully the razors before putting them back in their box:

"Now we can shake hands."

"I don't want to bother you..."

"Oh, come on!... Not only are you not bothering me, but I have something to speak with you about... But let me first put on my shirt."

He lifted, with care, above his head, a white shirt that he had just taken off the bed: his arms and neck bare, his fat belly sticking out under the flannel undershirt! Then, his head, buried, disappeared for a moment, in his very starched, rigid, and crackling dress shirt. I am still cannot get over it: him, speaking to me familiarly! He who, for over twelve years now, since the day Helen ran off and left him for Mr. de Vandeuilles, has always spoken to me formally. A simple distraction perhaps? An unconscious return to a habit of the past, acquired on school benches? Or a subtle way of letting me know that he was no longer cross with me, that I had sufficiently made up for my errors by helping him get back together again with his wife? Finally, he was going to have me appointed, I would see! And, at this moment, I felt for him a sort of immediate sympathy, a completely new feeling. For nothing at all, with a simple gesture, I would have helped him voluntarily get his neck free of that rigid dicky, tight as a piece of cardboard, which he was having a devil of a time trying not to break.

"There!" he said when, his shirt finally passed down over his neck, all he had left to do was button his sleeves; "I wanted to reproach you for something..."

"Reproach me?"

"Yes! Weren't you charged with composing my invitation list of guests for the soirée this evening?... Okay, then go and get that piece of paper there, in the office, on the bureau... and read it!"

The piece of paper contained a supplementary list of twenty names of notable people, whom, according to Moreau, I had had the unpardonable thoughtlessness of forgetting to invite: the sub clerk of the court, the two city librarians, the superior officers of the garrison regiment, etc. It had always been up to him, Moreau, to take care of everything by himself! To get along in this way with the most diverse details, my God! it was necessary to have one of those heads! And, unable to tie the knot in his white tie, Moreau rang for help. The domestic also helped him to put on his jacket. Once ready, satisfied doubtless after one glance at himself in the wardrobe mirror, where "the President" saw himself from head to toe, Moreau walked over to me.

"Now, my dear friend, I'm at your disposition!... Come, let's go into my office... We have a full quarter of an hour to kill..."

Sitting in his imposing Louis XIII armchair, he employed the quarter of an hour paring his nails with little scissors and probed me as to the arrangements that needed to be made "in order not to find ourselves completely unprepared when, in two and one half years from now, the current first president would reach the age limit..." Him! Moreau! first president in two and a half years! And why not? All the while answering softly his interested questions on the state of my relationships at the ministry, I summarized for myself what I had already done for this man: "Counselor in Algiers, when his wife had run off, him, because of me!... To the point of becoming president of the chamber in Algiers!... Then, president of the chamber here, thanks to my stepping down as counselor which was offered in exchange for the position of Attorney General..." What steps taken, what troubles, what bowing and scraping! And it wasn't over yet, I was ready to start anew. All this for Helen, who, on the floor below, ought to have finished her toilette by now. I looked at the pendulum in the clock. Great God! three minutes before seven o'clock! The first guests ought to have arrived by now, and me, instead of going to rejoin Helen, I was listening to Moreau!

"Very well!" I said rising to cut the conversation short. "We can speak of this again, but now it's time to go down."

"Time's always advancing!... We have time... Listen! I have a bright idea..."

But I looked at my wrist watch: "Look at that! seven fifteen!" And I walked toward the door all the same. So his bright idea and he followed me, walked down the staircase with me, slowed me down on each step: "It's necessary that, starting this coming spring, you make a first trip to Paris..." On the landing of the first floor, he held me back by the arm: "You do understand the importance, yes?..."

"Yes; consider me informed. Your idea is excellent. You may count on me... If you like, I could even come tomorrow morning to speak with you more about it, with a fresh mind."

"Come early!"

He let go of my arm finally.

Helen was in the salon, seated on one of the tête-à-tête sofas, next to the wife of the new public prosecutor, a little blond Normand woman, who looked younger than her age, but ugly, with a big mouth and thin, spiteful lips, with a nose stuck insolently in the air, and small, wily eyes, piercing like a gimlet. At the other end of the fireplace, the public prosecutor, in an armchair. Moreau had barely entered the room behind me when the door opened again, and the domestic announced:

"Mr. and Mrs. de Lancy."

Before the ceremonious salutations were completed, the little Normand woman, addressing herself to Mrs. de Lancy, said:

"Madam, help me out here; I'm in the process of saying something quite bad about your town." And, designating Helen, in the most hypocritically natural tone of voice, she said: "The Mrs., who knows Paris better than I do, does not wish to concur that there is Paris, and only Paris, in the world..."

A loaded pistol discharged two inches from my ear could not have more disagreeably flayed the tympanum than this phrase: "The Mrs., who knows Paris better than I do!" lobbed at Helen, straight in her face, in her own house. Instinctively, I looked at Helen. She was smiling. What was it that was so magnificent about her? Her hair or her look? Maybe her velvet black dress. She was smiling, and I was immediately put at ease. It was impossible to see this smile and not want to fall down at her knees. Mrs. de Lancy got up and went to sit down on a cushion in front of Helen, took her hand and held it in her own, asking her in a low voice how she was doing. I could have covered them in kisses, the long, surprisingly small, slender, pale, aristocratic fingers of Mrs. de Lancy.

The other guests arrived. The rector from the Academy, a general, the state prosecutor and the sub-prefect, one right after the other nearly. The first president and his wife were the last ones to arrive.

"Dinner is served," we were told.

Now we dined. No general conversation during the potage, nor during the entrée. Barely a few words in hushed voices, between those sitting next to each other, and on generalities. Winter was going to be cold; the swallows had departed early and those with delicate constitutions ought to take precautions. There were several cases of typhoid fever at the end of summer. An itinerant troupe of entertainers would, in eight days, perform *Bourgeois de Pont-Arcy*. After that, only the subdued sound of forks, flat dishes, some plates relocated on the table in precaution, the unfortunate bumping of a glass with its ensuing vibrations immediately quieted with a finger; and the hushed offers by domestics: "Salmon... Some bread... Madera?" Then the tail ends of discreet conversations developed into new ones: Mr. de Lancy had spent less time hunting on his lands than in previous years! That Sardou, of the French Academy, was truly a man of the theater, intimately familiar with the human heart and its furthest recesses. Mrs. de Lancy spoke in general about her son Henry, recently nominated lieutenant of the reserve. The new public prosecutor moaned over the state of French belle-lettres; since the appearance of *Notre-Dame de Paris*, he hadn't read a single novel! Each time he had come across one at home he burned it!

"He's a Saracen, your husband!" murmured

the rector, a man of spirit, into the ear of the public prosecutor's wife.

She opened her little eyes as widely as possible.

"Yes," continued the rector, "because he burns books!... The Saracens, didn't they burn the Library of Alexandria?"

But Mr. de Lancy, who had heard him, stopped short in the middle of a demonstration he was giving to the sub-prefect, on the possibility of establishing local horse races, provided the government would assist with it. And, a bit warmed up already by the first glasses of wine, always seizing in mid-flight the opportunity of launching into a joke, he addressed himself very loudly to the little Normand woman:

"Mrs., how did you find l'*Assommoir*?"[5]

This elicited a discreet "oh!", accompanied here and there at the table by suppressed bursts of laughter that just kept going. And Moreau, in the capacity of master of the house, felt it his responsibility to reprimand Mr. de Lancy, while reserving for himself the rights of determining what was in good taste and of moral character. But the ice had been broken. Besides, they were at the roast meat now, the Corton[6] and the Chambertin[7] was passed around. And from the topic of literature the conversation slid into poli-

---

[5]l'*Assommoir*: a novel, written by Émile Zola and published in 1877, about a woman protagonist who descends into alcoholism and homelessness.

[6]Corton: a Burdundian white wine of high repute.

tics. Everything was going badly! French society was lost! Since the abortion on May 16, the Marshal was only making things worse![8] And, as the general, with a mouth full of food, rolled his terrible eyes and raised energetically his shoulders in a demonstration of defense of his Marshal, the new public prosecutor repeated at each instant, with a profound air, "There are no more men!" The phrase seemed hard for the sub-prefect to swallow, who, lacking an easy elocution, stammered a little in objection that, nevertheless, in the new administration, among his colleagues recently appointed to the business of public affairs... And, as the sentence dragged on, the hot-headed Mr. de Lancy intervened:

"On May 16, they lacked energy; and if I had been on hand instead of those idiots, de Fourtou and de Broglie, me!..."

That did it: the heads looked up; the gentlemen's voices, growing louder and more heated, cut each other off, crossed each other, while the ladies, no longer listening, their plate empty, fanned themselves lightly, some of them sitting back in their chair. Helen, herself, responded from time to time to a starchy phrase of the first president, who was sitting on her right; then, with a glance at the domestics, she urged more attention be paid to the service which was languishing. Suddenly, at dessert, at the moment of champagne, they heard soft music that seemed to de-

---

[7]Chambertin: a Burgundian red wine of high repute.

[8]May 16, 1877: when then President of the Third Republic, Marshal MacMahon, dissolved French parliament after the Chamber passed a vote of no confidence.

scend from the ceiling. The orchestra, already installed on the platform in the dance room upstairs, was performing the first waltz.

"Good! we will be dancing soon!" said Mr. de Lancy.

And he put his champagne glass down, where the foam of the Moët was dying down, in order to clap his two hands together, one against the other, like a big child.

"To dine with music! Fi, then!" the wife of the new public prosecutor said, sniggering.

"Just like in Paris, at the Palais-Royal!" whispered the rector to her.

"Yes... in '47!"

I stopped listening to them. And nobody paid any more attention to the waltz. In front of me, the long, thin fingers of Mrs. de Lancy peeled a mandarin, whose delicate, penetrating, and fine odor I could smell from across the table. And me, I sat there asking myself if somewhere, sometime, I had not heard that same tune played in triple-time. While I was racking my memory, my eyes crossed those of Helen. The same thought! On her face, a sudden flush. She was trying to remember like me. It must have been the same waltz. The one that played eternally on the street organ, on the boulevard des Batignolles, while Fernand, the acrobat in flesh-colored undershirt and cherry-red shorts lifted a barrel with his teeth.

Fernand! And Helen, waiting for the street performer on the exterior boulevard; and Fernand, holding his arm around her waist on the rue de Rome; my night of torture spent in the room of the town-house, waiting by the window, my interrogating the black void of the Cité-des-Fleurs, a fever leading me hour after hour back to my table where I covered sheets of writing paper with incoherent phrases, – all that came back to me at once, in a second, with the shivering thought that the interrupted nightmare might start all over again. But, at the very moment of this sudden malaise, wasn't it time for us to rise from the table? I had just seen this same Helen rise first among them, pass on the arm of the first president in front of her guests, who were on their feet and re-spectful. Now, in the three rooms filled with enchant-ment, the entire "high society" of X*** arrived in sin-gle file, all following Helen's lead: the ladies with their low necklines, a little touched, dazzled by the bright lights, overwhelmed by the luxury, the rank and the fortune, wondering whether their toilette was irreproachable and if Mrs. Moreau was still upset with them; the gentlemen bowing to her very low. Look at that! over there, what do you see? That long woman straight as a board, so poorly dressed, and her head well above the others, it was unbelievable! "Mrs. Jauffret!" murmured everyone. Embarrassed by her height, feeling all eyes upon her, the surprised looks that seemed to say: "How's that? She dared to come to this house that used to belong to her!... Her good little man, already at the gambling table, tries to win back enough money to pay for his wife's toilette!" – awkward up there and looking surly, Mrs.

Jauffret could not find a chair. The wife of the new prosecutor made a sign to her, from afar, that there was a place to sit beside her. And they began to whisper to each other, very animated, their eyes looking at Helen from time to time. But the muted hatred of their two looks went unnoticed amidst the brouhaha of joviality of a town whose heart had been won back. Happy for Helen, definitively reassured, I felt very warm. I went to find refuge in the little blue room.

There, the light was dimmer, the temperature cooler. No more than four whist players at a table, with some men standing, turning their back to me, placing bets on each trick. The tête-á-tête where Helen sits in the afternoon, embroidering or reading, was empty. I sat down there, feeling very tired, and, taking out my handkerchief, I wiped my forehead and cheeks. A domestic passed by with a tray. I took a sorbet. Then, feeling restored, I sat back, feet on the stool, head leaning against the back of the tête-á-tête. The murmur of the quadrille that the orchestra was playing at that moment in the ballroom seemed very far away. One would have said that there was a party in some house next door, while the Moreau chalet slept, plunged in habitual calm. And I began to think back on the several silent hours passed one on one with Helen, – with Helen recovered from Paris the day after that terrible night, and escorted by me, almost in spite of herself, into an unknown village in the hinterlands of Brittany... "Five *louis* for Mr. Jauffret? – I have them!" responded one of the gamblers in a small voice. And the new cards, dealt out one by one, were distributed with small dry slapping sounds. There, on the beach, it was the rhythmical beating of the swell pounding against the sonorous cliff, then dripping away, foamy among the pebbles. And Helen, completely dejected, her eyes sunken and red after many nights of insomnia, passed drab afternoons; some book, which she didn't read, open in her lap; looking with a fixed gaze, at into the horizon, without thinking about anything and without seeing anything. Me, a little to the side, absorbed apparently in a journal, trying to make myself forget that I would have liked nothing more than to be a dog lying at her feet, pretending to sleep, all the while looking up at her. Happy nevertheless, progressing quietly in the background on projects that I kept to myself and did not want her to suspect, I waited... All of a sudden, my eyelids closed. I stopped hearing the distant orchestra, the sliding of new cards across the table. I had fallen asleep!... But Helen was always there, sitting in front of the Ocean. And me, or rather, another me whom I have never been, young and strong, for the first time in my life, I held her in my arms and pressed her against my chest: "I love you!" And she, her bosom swollen with emotion and with desire, struggled; then, in the middle of her resistance, I felt her two arms, as if moved by a will other than her own, join together behind me and pull me closer to her. "Helen, be mine, finally, Helen!" I wanted to cry out; but, from the bottom of my chest swollen with desires, before the words could reach my lips, they had turned into a groan of intense pleasure... All of a sudden, a hand, laid gently on my shoulder, woke me.

"It's you, Helen!" I said, very surprised. "What time is it?"

"It's almost five o'clock, my friend."

"Five o'clock!"

The table of whist was still there, with two candles burning right down to the candle ring. One of the two lampshades just then caused wax to splatter on the green tablecloth. And the players had disappeared, leaving their blue cards jumbled together with the white ones.

"You were snoring loudly," Helen said to me; "I was afraid to disturb you... You know, everyone has gone."

"It's not possible!"

And I rose from the chair, very sheepishly.

"You won't go home on foot," she responded. "It snowed all last night and it's very cold outside... We'll hitch up the horses."

Then, as I was remonstrating, she added:

"You will drink a bowl of hot bouillon, – I want you to, before you go. And, you know, given you are subject to pains... You will wrap your shoulders with this large shawl of mine..."

* * *

I won't return to the chalet for another few days. I will have Nanon go there and return the flannel shawl to her for me.

Other Books by the Publisher

Fanchette's Pretty Little Foot by Restif de la Bretonne

Je M'Accuse... by Léon Bloy

My Hospitals & My Prisons by Paul Verlaine

Salvation Through the Jews by Léon Bloy

Words of a Demolitions Contractor by Léon Bloy

Cellulely by Paul Verlaine

Ecclesiastical Laurels by Jacques Rochette de la Morlière

Flowers of Bitumen by Émile Goudeau

Songs for Her & Odes in Her Honor by Paul Verlaine

On Huysmans' Tomb by Léon Bloy

Ten Years a Bohemian by Émile Goudeau

The Soul of Napoleon by Léon Bloy

Blood of the Poor by Léon Bloy

Joan of Arc and Germany by Léon Bloy

A Platonic Love by Paul Alexis

The Revealer of the Globe: Christopher Columbus & His Future Beatification (Part One) by Léon Bloy

An Immodest Proposal by Dr. Helmut Schleppend

The Pornographer by Restif de la Bretonne

Style (Theory and History) by Ernest Hello

On the Threshold of the Apocalypse: 1913-1915 by Léon Bloy

She Who Weeps (Our Lady of La Salette) by Léon Bloy

The Sylph by Claude Prosper Jolyot de Crébillon (*fils*)

Voyage in France by a Frenchman by Paul Verlaine

Ourigan, Oregon by William Clark, Richard Robinson, and anonymous

Drowning by Yu Dafu

Cull of April by Francis Vielé-Griffin

The Misfortune of Monsieur Fraque by Paul Alexis

Fêtes Galantes & Songs Without Words by Paul Verlaine

Joys by Francis Vielé-Griffin

The Son of Louis XVI by Léon Bloy

Septentrion by Jean Raspail

The Resurrection of Villiers de l'Isle-Adam by Léon Bloy

Poems Saturnian by Paul Verlaine

The Biography of Léon Bloy: Memories of a Friend by René Martineau

Fredegund, France: A Book of Poetry by Richard Robinson

The Good Song by Paul Verlaine

Swans by Francis Vielé-Griffin

Constantinople and Byzantium by Léon Bloy

Enamels and Cameos by Théophile Gautier

Four Years of Captivity in Cochons-sur-Marne: 1900-1904 by Léon Bloy

Dark Minerva: Prolegomena: The Moral Construction of Dante's Divine Comedy by Giovanni Pascoli

What is Fascism: Discourses and Polemics by Giovanni Gentile

The Desperate Man by Léon Bloy

Meditations of a Solitary in 1916 by Léon Bloy

The Ride of Yeldis & Other Poems by Francis Vielé-Griffin

Silvie & The Chimeras by Gérard de Nerval

Italian Nationalism by Enrico Corradini

A Silver-Grey Death and *Drowning* by Yu Dafu

Doctrines of Hatred, Part I: Anti-Semitism by Anatole Leroy-Beaulieu

Rhymes of Joy by Théodore Hannon

Windows and Doors by Richard Robinson

The Perverted Peasant by Restif de la Bretonne

Early Poetry by Auguste de Villiers de l'Isle-Adam

Antisthenes: The Founder of Cynicism by Charles Chappuis

The Ungrateful Beggar by Léon Bloy

Great Men Are Slain Here by Léon Bloy

Fallacies: Part 3, Book 4 of Summa Logicae by William of Ockham